TIME ZONE

The chance to go back and fix one fatal mistake

RV Hodge

Books by RV Hodge
www.thervhodge.com

Dedicated to my parents, Bob and Darlene Hodge,

whose influence on me has transcended time.

– RV

TIME ZONE

by RV Hodge

Bad ...

I landed facedown on the cold floor. The crashing jail cell door reverberated violently, and then all was silent except for a persistent drip. I assumed that came from the tiny sink in the corner. The place smelled like an animal cage that needed to be cleaned. I tried to move. Everything hurt.

I probably shouldn't have fought against those guys, I mused, reflecting on how I had frantically struggled against the two burly guards. At that point there was nothing I could have gained. But what it got me was cussed, kidney punched, and body slammed through the doorway.

"They must have been holding back on account of my age," I moaned under my breath.

My anger dried up quickly. But I was still desperate. I was especially desperate.

Urgently, my mind raced through my plight. *What am I now? Sixty-seven? I hate this instant-aging thing. And they've got my phone. I've got to get the phone and get out of here. But then where? I'm running out of safe places.*

My mind flitted around out of control for a few minutes. The sound of the cell door replayed in my memory, and I mused wryly, *At least that sound is constant. Well, everywhere I've been so far.* It made no logical sense, but I found some consolation in the consistency.

When I finally mustered the willpower to push myself up to my knees, it was abundantly clear that the age factor was not working in my favor. I attempted to reach where the TASER had bit into my back. I was certain it was still bleeding. It was not.

Another irony struck me: *Those things seem to be getting hotter every time I get hit with one. Or maybe,* I considered, *that's an age thing too.*

As I cataloged my sources of pain, a nagging concern surfaced. *Why had I not been read my Miranda Rights?*

It was disconcerting that the police had been dismissive, even contemptuous, of the notion of any suspects' rights. I wondered if that was a sign of the times or if the officer had taken it personally when I had yanked his TASER and tried to use it against him. I made a mental note not to do that again. It was too bad, as that had worked particularly well a couple of times in the past. I muttered to myself, "Electric shielding incorporated into body armor. It's brilliant. Why didn't I invent that one?"

With some effort, I reached for the corner of the cot in the cell and gingerly pulled myself to my feet. It was more difficult than I had anticipated. But once I got straightened up, I found myself face-to-face with my own reflection in the polished stainless steel that passed for a mirror. I looked like something an alley cat had regurgitated.

The shock of that view drove home an agonizing realization: I had failed.

I put my hands on the wall on either side of the mirror and leaned my forehead against my reflection. It was cool against my skin. I felt like crying. "I'm sorry, Farren," I whispered. And I knew at that moment there was no longer any possibility that I could rescue him.

Then my mind briefly skipped back to the day that Ellen had died. In a flashback, I relived that nightmare for several surreal seconds before I stuffed it back into the recesses of my memory. It had been a fool's hope to try to undo that day. Again I whispered, "I've failed you too."

I tried to force myself to rationally assess my current predicament. There was no denying that I had been flirting with death at every jump. And at that moment, my reflection candidly affirmed that I had flirted too much.

"It's 2046. You're sixty-seven years old," I accused my reflection. "Beat up. Locked up … again. And if you go any further, you're going to get yourself killed too. Idiot."

As I tried to comb my hair down with my fingers, I muttered, "But you're not going anywhere without your phone."

Then, for the hundredth time, I asked myself, "Am I completely insane? Maybe I do belong in a psych ward."

The old man in the mirror did not reply, but the look of defeat was an unmistakable indictment. In despair I chided, "They've got your phone. They're going to set off World War III."

Slowly I backed away from the mirror as if it might jump me when I turned my back. Carefully, I sat down on the edge of the bunk and, as I leaned back, my head cracked against the steel frame of the bunk above. "Ugh! This really isn't my day," I hissed through gritted teeth.

Someone tapped my arm, and I jumped straight up, busting my head on the upper bunk a second time before piling up on the floor. I hate to think what I said then.

Shakily I clamored to my feet and saw my cellmate, who looked like a hobo. "My bunk, old-timer. Get your own," he snapped as he rudely gestured up.

Standing there, holding onto the frame of the upper bunk, I felt my heart pounding too fast. My knees felt like jelly, and for a moment I was afraid I might have a heart attack. I gasped, "Sorry, man. I never even knew anyone else was in here, but you about scared the life out of me!"

The hobo muttered, "Yeah, yeah. You and your buddies got a lot going on there. Just keep what's in your head inside your head."

Looking at the top bunk, I briefly considered lying back down on the floor. But getting up from the floor had been hard enough the first two times. So, with an embarrassing amount of moaning and groaning, I climbed into the upper bunk, and flopped onto the hard mattress like it was made of the finest goose down. In about two seconds, I heard the hobo snoring.

Desperately I thought, *I've got to get out of this place!*

And for the millionth time, I wondered if my time exposure was limited or had an expiration.

I thought about my friend Farren, and I knew logically that he had to be dead. I wondered if there was a limit to how much time I had before I actually could not save him. I whispered to myself, "That's assuming that it's reversible to begin with. And the sad irony is, Farren was probably the only person on earth who could have done the math to even determine if that theory was viable."

My mind raced over what I had been through in the past few days. Or actually, the past half century, to be technically correct.

In early middle school, I had formulated a theory that there was a measurable correlation between the frequency signatures of matter and time and space. I was certain that Einstein would have approved of all of that. I wished I had consulted him first. As my research progressed, I further postulated that by manipulating those unique frequencies, either time or space could be affected. I was eventually rewarded with the astonishing discovery that I could change both time and space based on a predictable sequence of frequency variances.

With a curse, the hobo kicked the bottom of my bunk, scaring me half out of my life a second time. Apparently I had been thinking out loud.

"Man, you got to stop doing that!" I shouted.

The hobo snapped back, "You got to quit talking to yourself. There ain't no committee meeting in here! I'm trying to sleep!"

Suddenly I had inspiration. I asked the hobo, "Hey, they didn't read me my Miranda Rights. What do I have to do to get a legal counselor?"

The hobo laughed, and mocked, "Do much vintage television, do we?"

"What? We don't have Miranda Rights?" I asked incredulously.

The hobo snorted. "They haven't had that abusive system since I was, like, ten. What? Have you been living under a log or something?"

"Abusive system?" I sputtered.

The hobo smirked, "You done the crime, you gonna do the time."

"Well, I haven't 'done the crime' until I've been found guilty by a jury of my peers," I said, doubting the outcome of everything at that moment.

Again the guy snorted. "Yeah, well, if that's what ticks your pacemaker, keep on living in that world. Just do it quiet."

I wanted to correct his grammar, but decided against it. My mind raced. Things had changed a lot. "How long will it be before I see a judge?" I asked.

"Depends on what you done," the hobo responded. Then with an exasperated sigh, he muttered, "You don't get this quiet thing, do you?"

I replied, "I was arrested for trespassing." I hesitated to add the location, but decided to share it in the hope of learning how to deal with the new norm. I added, "In a research facility. But I used to work there, so I really wasn't trespassing."

To my surprise, the hobo climbed out of his bunk. He was younger than I had expected. After looking me over with a sense of curiosity, he said, "You're keeping something back from your story, because there's no way to get past security into someplace that could get you arrested. You used a weapon? Or took a hostage?"

Hobo's leading questions rubbed me the wrong direction. He gave me the impression of a gossip looking for a juicy morsel.

"No weapons. It's a really long story," I answered curtly.

The guy mumbled, "They'll process you in a month or so. Maybe quicker after your little temper tantrum at the door here." He seemed disappointed with my explanation.

"A month!" I blurted. "I haven't got a month!"

The hobo shook his head with resignation as he replied, "Buddy, you got a year, at least. It ain't all bad. I'm two months in, waiting for my hearing. Public drunkenness will get you half a year of free room and board. Beats sleeping under a bridge."

Hobo paused, then added as an afterthought, "At least you didn't resist arrest."

Fear choked up in my throat. Slowly I replied, "I kind of grabbed one of the cop's TASERs and fired on him."

The hobo squinted his eyes and looked at me with a fresh interest. "You really ain't too bright, are you, old-timer?" he asked rhetorically.

I had a sudden urge to defend myself and recite my list of degrees. But I thought, *I'm the one who is clueless here. And besides that, this guy is a veteran of the current system, and I need him to tell me what's going on.* Instead I asked, "How bad is it going to be?"

The hobo just shrugged his shoulders and replied, "They get excited about that kind of stuff. They'll process you within an hour. And you're gonna die in this place."

At that point, I almost panicked. The fear was trying to migrate from my throat to my chest as I asked the guy, "Is there any way I can plead this with a judge?"

The guy gave me a sidelong look of empathy and said, "Unless you're made out of money, pal, you see the processing D.A., and that's the last time you see the light of day."

Despondently I flopped back down on the pillow. I heard the hobo get back into his bunk, and had a moment of secret envy at his ability to unconditionally accept his circumstances.

"I've got to get my phone," I muttered softly. "One hour. Maybe less than an hour. I've got to get out of this place. How much can I tell them and not get locked up in the psych ward? I've got to get my phone. Maybe the D.A. will let me show him my phone."

In my mind, only about three minutes had passed when two guards showed up at the door. One of them held a

TASER at the ready. The other passed an orange jumpsuit through the slot in the door. *The fashion never seems to change,* I mused.

Submissively, I went to the door and tried to sound rational, but my voice probably sounded more like I was whimpering. I said, "Listen. This is going to be really hard to explain. But it's imperative that I talk to someone in the judicial system. I have some highly-classified information that can't be talked about in an open court setting."

The guards laughed. The one with the TASER demanded, "Change out, you got one minute, unless you want to get zapped in your all-unders." He sounded a bit too eager to me.

I hastily changed into the jumpsuit. I did not like the image that conjured in my mind of how bad it would feel to get tazed with bare feet on a metal floor. They instructed me to put my old clothes in a bag, and my name and the number on my jumpsuit was written on the bag.

One of the guards sarcastically remarked, "At least your clothes are already out-of-date. Maybe they'll be back in style when you get 'em back!" They opened the door and, with the TASER sight trained on the center of my chest, I submitted to being manacled.

It was a pretty serious set of manacles. I guessed that they must have read my arrest report. At that point, I earnestly regretted biting the arresting officer on the ear.

As they led me out, my hobo cellmate called out, "Take that peach cobbler to the psych unit. Don't bring him back here! He's a nut! He thinks he's from another planet. And he won't shut up!"

The cell door closed on Hobo's rant, with me on the outside that time. I asked, "Peach cobbler?"

One of the guards slapped me on the back and chortled, "In your day, Grandpa, they would have called you a fruitcake!"

Justice

Waiting my turn in line to see the processor, I realized just how grim the situation was. I had often wished that justice was as swift and decisive as I was witnessing at that moment. *This isn't looking good,* I reflected anxiously. The sentences were handed out at a rate of about one per minute. And everyone in line received a guilty verdict. There was not a hint of 'innocent until proven guilty' in that courtroom.

The line moved quickly, and it did not take long before I was standing in front of the processor.

He was a sharply-dressed young fellow, and I wondered if he got paid on commission. Wisely, I kept that comment to myself. Trying to use timing to my advantage, as soon as he opened my file, I made my plea. I knew I only had sixty seconds. I said, "Sir, I have some seriously important classified information that needs to be shared with someone either with a high security clearance level in the government or the research world. And I could show you something on my phone that would prove that to you without revealing any sensitive classified secrets."

The man never looked up. He grabbed a stamp, stamped my file, and handed it to the bailiff. *Twenty-eight seconds!* I mentally gasped.

I could not help but notice that the ink was green. I had seen a lot of blacks, and one red. I had presumed the blacks were assigned prison terms, and the red was probably a death sentence. Before I could ask, the bailiff gleefully called out, "First green of the night."

My guards laughed. And one of them cheerily said, "It's been a slow night for the doctor." Then, without any further ado, I was ushered out a doorway that I had not seen anyone else go through.

We passed by several cells, and I craned to glance through one of the small windows on a door. Confirming my deepest fear, I saw that the rooms were padded. My heart sank. I had been sentenced to the psychiatric unit.

I was led into a stark room and unceremoniously deposited in a chair at a small table, with a conspicuously empty chair on the other side. The steel manacles were replaced with a padded fabric version of the same, but with mitten ends, which prevented me from reaching the Velcro fasteners. Then, to my astonishment, the guards left me alone in the room.

As the door closed, an automatic deadbolt snapped decisively into place. Alone for the first time in several hours, I hung my head in dread. At that moment I felt alienated from the entire world.

In the adjacent room, I could hear the pixelated voice of one of the guards say, "Dr. Blake, we've got your first victim of the night." The sound was muted by the wall, but clear enough to send a chill down my spine.

There was no sound for several minutes, then the other door opened. The distinct sound of women's shoes clicked on the tile, and I glanced sideways in surprise.

How did I recognize that sound? I wondered as I watched the approaching feet. They stopped at the edge of the table and, apprehensively, I looked up into the eyes of a stern-faced woman.

She appeared to be in her mid-sixties and was shorter than my imagination had made her out to be.

For some reason I had an irrational urge to decode her racial heritage. Her eyes and cheekbone structure told me she was part Oriental or possibly Alaskan Native. The dark skin threw me off, and I reasoned there had to be either some African or Jamaican heritage as well. Whatever the combination was, I thought it had worked out pretty well. I mused, *She must have been quite the looker when she was young.*

My reverie was suddenly interrupted when I realized she was speaking to me.

Visibly irritated by my inattention, Dr. Blake repeated, "So, what is it you've done, Mr. Thompson?"

She was glancing through my file as she asked, and I knew she was just testing my grip on reality. It was clear that this woman had heard it all, and had probably already decided my fate.

I began to explain. "I used to work for EXL Lab, and I've made a remarkable and somewhat scary discovery. In my panicked haste to get in and speak to someone, I managed to get myself into big trouble, and really good and arrested." Dr. Blake smiled a little, which confused me. Weakly, I commented, "I didn't think what I'd said was that amusing."

The doctor looked up at me with a grin and replied, "Aren't you a bit old to be tussling with police officers?"

I just shrugged and went straight to the point. "If I could show you my phone ... If you would let me access my phone, I could show you that I need to speak to somebody at a high security clearance level. And if you don't believe me, you can lock me up, and I won't say another word about it."

She stared at me for a long minute, and picked up what looked like a pen. It turned out to be some kind of a phone or radio. With it, she called for my personal belongings. There was a brief discussion about 'the weapon,' which puzzled me, until I realized they were talking about my Leatherman. In a few minutes, my personal effects, minus my Leatherman, were brought into the room. While we had been waiting, I had attempted to strike up a conversation with Dr. Blake, but she did not take the bait. When we were again left alone, she picked up my phone and examined it in awe. Finally she said, "You've been carrying this relic around for a long time, Mr. Thompson."

I looked at her weakly and said, "Probably not for nearly as long as you might imagine."

She just shook her head and asked, "What's your password?"

I replied, "It's 87 digits long, and requires my right index finger biometric input."

She read the note on the bag that it had been delivered in. It turned out she could be expressive after all. Her eyebrows arched high as she commented, "That would explain why Crypto couldn't crack into it." She looked at my hand muzzles and warned, "This room is visually monitored on camera, and there is a trigger-happy guard outside the door. If you do anything remotely suspicious, he'll come through that door and shoot you dead."

"Yes, Ma'am," I replied.

She gave me a sharp look and said, "Don't call me 'Ma'am.' "

I was tempted to comment about her age, but then realized we were about the same. I blinked back my thoughts and just nodded. I also pinned her accent to Charleston, South Carolina.

Carefully she uncuffed the mitten part of my right hand. I had a sudden sense of guarded relief, and quickly began to enter my password. I was focusing on my screen, but in my peripheral vision, I could see that she was openly amused.

In an attempt to buy time, I made a running monologue about the sensitive nature of what I was about to show her. As I pulled up the EXL app, I had to make the instantaneous decision of where and when to jump. I decided to go back to college. I entered May 18, 1999, then I entered the coordinates, to the best of my recollection, of my dorm room. I anxiously hoped it was the right room, but I did not have much time to second-guess myself.

A quick glance at the screenshot verified that it looked right, at least it seemed so after seventeen years. *Or,* I mused wryly, *was it actually forty-six years?*

I suddenly was filled with empathy for Dr. Blake, because she had been the first person who had even remotely attempted to help me. I said, "Dr. Blake, I want to thank you very much for being so understanding. You have undoubtedly saved my life, and may have saved the life of my best friend. And possibly, if I can undo everything I've done, you may have averted a global war." As my finger touched the purple button, I felt the all-too-familiar static shock enter my hand as my molecular frequency was modified to that of a different time and place. But I also felt a completely unfamiliar sensation on my left shoulder.

Brown University

I landed hard on the dorm room floor. My first thought was, *How many times am I going to do that before I remember to not lean on something when I'm changing time zones?*

A woman's voice screamed, "Guard!" then abruptly stopped. I could feel her pushing away from me as she jumped to her feet. Confused, I glanced over my shoulder. She was holding her pen-phone with a look of stark terror on her face. "Oh! My! Gosh!" she exclaimed. "What have you done to me? What have you done to you? What have you done?"

In the calmest voice I could muster, I screamed, "Why did you touch me?"

With a mixture of anger and bewilderment, I again demanded, "Why did you touch me?" I was on the verge of tears.

"Why did you lie to me?" she demanded in retort. She looked as if she was about to cry as well. Only it looked like hers was due to anger.

I looked at her for a long moment, mouth agape, and finally found the words. "Because you wouldn't have believed me anyway. And now you've exponentially complicated my whole mission!"

"Change us back!" she demanded. "Change us back, or so help me, I'll stab you with this phone!"

"Uncuff me!" I replied hotly, as I desperately tried to reach the Velcro with my free finger. "We've time jumped! I'll take you back if you uncuff me now!" I desperately wanted to be rid of her.

"Take us back, then I'll uncuff you!" she insisted.

"You're stuck right here with me until you uncuff me!"
I shouted. I fancied my argument was ironclad in my
frenzied state of mind.

She gestured frantically with the phone-pen, "Have you
drugged me? That is a capital crime! **What** have you
done to me?"

"You've killed my friend," I accused illogically. And as
the idiocy of my words sank in, I amended my
accusation to a plea. "You're at least keeping me from
going and rescuing him. You've got to uncuff me.
Please!"

"Mr. Thompson, you are a convicted felon, in my
custody, and I am obligated to keep you confined," she
replied hotly.

Something clicked inside my head, and I suddenly
became rational. I leaned back against the bed and said
calmly, "And we're not going anywhere." Then, before I
could logically process what I saw, the words came out
of my mouth, "Something's wrong about this room."

Dr. Blake lunged at me with the phone-pen. As we
tussled on the floor, she screamed incoherently and tried
to stab me. I threw my cuffed arms up to protect myself
from her tirade, and I heard my own voice yelling. It
seemed like it lasted a long time, but it had probably
only been a few seconds, when we both somehow heard
the key enter the lock on the door. We both stopped
yelling and looked with rapt horror at the door as it
swung open.

Lars was obviously in shock as he registered the scene.
His wide eyes punctuated his normally very pale face,
which had turned deep red. He blurted, in his thick
Swedish accent, "Tanya! I didn't realize you two knew
each other." He backed out the door, as he stammered,
"I would not have thought either of you were into that
kind of ... um, stuff."

The door clicked closed and the lock bolted shut. And
we both spoke at the same time. In stunned disbelief,
she asked, "You're Lars' roommate?" And I asked,
"Tanya? How does he even know you?"

Dr. Blake jumped up, and it was obvious she had been slimmer in her younger years. She held up her sagging pants and, in that moment, we both realized the profound awkwardness of how we looked. She blurted, "You went to Brown University?"

I looked at her for a second and retorted, "You went to Brown University?"

"Class of 2001," she replied hesitantly as her eyes darted around the room suspiciously.

"I guess technically I graduated tomorrow," I responded.

With her hand on her forehead, Dr. Blake bemoaned, "This is not good." Her words were fringed with panic. "Not good. Oh, no! Now Lars thinks we're into ..."

Cutting her off, I shook my head. "This all goes away. Listen! I know, this is .... Wait! I don't know Lars. My roommate ... was Farren." My mind swirled and her panic infected me instantly. Breathlessly I whispered, "Oh my gosh. It's retroactive."

Dr. Blake knelt down in front of me, looked me square in the face, and quietly but firmly demanded, "Explain to me exactly what is going on. I don't know how you're making all this ... stuff ... happen, but you'd better talk fast."

I felt hot tears running down my cheeks as I could not comprehend how Farren's death in the future changed his past. I heard my voice breaking up as I explained. "I'm a time jumper ... I guess."

She gave me a skeptical glare and asked, "Time jumper? Like you expect me to believe we are actually in the past?"

I shrugged and gestured around the room. "The only things in this room that are out of place came with us."

Her eyes narrowed and she asked, "So I could walk to that phone and call my mother, and she would still be alive?"

I nodded, but cautioned, "Any contact will complicate things ... a lot."

Tears welled in her eyes and she looked at the phone long enough that I expected her to make the call. When she looked back to me, she hoarsely whispered, "If this is some kind of trick ...."

I shook my head. "No trick," I replied softly.

Dr. Blake deliberately walked to the phone and took it off the hook. Her eyebrows went up and she remarked, "An actual dial tone." Then she dialed a number and, as it rang through, I had the terrifying notion that she was calling the police. But before I could say anything she said, "Hello ... Mom?"

The look of astonishment on her face told me she had connected with her mother. They spoke briefly in Japanese before she hung up the phone. Turning back to face me, there were tears in her eyes. Hoarsely she asked, "What is really going on here? This is not funny."

"I'm sorry, Dr. Blake. It's real," I replied. "My friend Farren decided he would make his first time jump into the future to see the Quincentennial fireworks at Independence Hall. That would be July 4, 2276."

Absently she interrupted me with, "I know what quincentennial means."

I nodded and continued, "I chose to go back and fix a ... a mistake ... a really terrible mistake in my past." I paused to control my tumultuous emotions. "That's when I discovered that, when time jumping, we age according to the chronological year into which we are landing. That's why we look like our youthful selves right ... now."

I trailed off as Dr. Blake seemed to be in somewhat of a trance. She muttered distantly, "I can't believe I got to hear her voice one more time." After a brief pause, she seemed to come back to our conversation and, wiping the tears from her cheeks, asked, "Your friend traveled so far into the future that survival was not possible?"

"I rushed back in hopes of stopping him, but he was gone already," I explained. "And so far, everything I've done has created more problems. What I really need to do is go back to the minute before each of the events

I've disrupted and replay them the way they were originally done in history."

"Can't you just call him back with the machine?" she asked, gesturing at my phone.

I replied, "We made two. I can't affect his with mine at all."

She looked at me with a different look, and mused aloud, "You made them?"

Absently, I replied, "Hardware, physics, and electronics. Farren was the genius behind the software and mathematics."

"Quite the mad scientist," she muttered, shaking her head.

"I hear that all the time," I acknowledged with a sigh. Then to my astonishment, she reached out and started unstrapping the Velcro. I looked up at her and said, "You need to come up with a good cover story, because I'm going to disappear the instant I drop you back at your office, and I wouldn't want you to get in trouble for helping me."

She was nodding. "I'm working on it," she said, then asked, "Where are you going?"

"I need a safe place to try and sort this all out. Someplace unaffected by all my jump disasters. I hate to think of all the zones where the police are searching for me. Anyway, I'm thinking I'll jump back to my own office in my real time. My natural time zone. Somehow I need to figure out how to get a couple hundred years into the future without vaporizing, then try to bring my friend Farren back. Unfortunately, he's probably the only man alive, or who was alive, who could figure out the math to make it all happen. Then," I muttered pensively, "I need to untangle my mess."

Dr. Blake looked at me and asked, "Was Farren a tall skinny guy with a thick unibrow?" She gestured with her finger as she asked.

"Yeah," I replied. "Everybody knew him as 'The Math Nerd'."

"I remember him," she replied.

I nodded. "He really stood out." Then I asked, "Are you ready to go back, Dr. Blake?"

"Just call me Tanya," she replied. Then, with a resigned sigh, she said, "Yes. Yes, I guess I'm ready."

It was an amazing relief in my mind to be able to discuss my time jumping troubles with someone who actually listened. Up to that moment, every single attempt had gotten me arrested, tazed, or shot at. I looked at Tanya through different eyes. *She was pretty hot back then,* I mused. *How did I manage to miss her?*

"Better grab your pen and your cuffs. We don't need to leave any more trouble behind," I instructed absently as I was keying in the information.

She gathered up all of the stray items that had come with us. And I pressed the button.

Sweet Home

We landed in Dr. Blake's interrogation room at exactly sixty seconds before we disappeared. As soon as we landed, Tanya said, "Let me get all of your things so there's no evidence here." And she called for my Leatherman.

When all of my belongings were in front of me, I expected her to say goodbye. What she said was, "Don't lean on the table." I smiled as I pressed the button. In the split second before I jumped time zones, I realized I was going to miss Tanya.

My landing was almost perfect in my own office chair. I still crashed to the floor, but it was really close. Tanya helped me up, and I gasped, "Why did you touch me?"

"You never told me your name," she answered.

"Chad," I replied.

Tanya nodded. "I know. I actually think I can help you."

I looked at her curiously. Secretly I was glad she was there, but I could not fathom how she could possibly help. I said, "I don't think there's any psychological factors involved in the time zone jumping."

But she was not listening. She held up the nameplate from my desk, and asked, "Dr. Thompson?" and gave me a sideways look of surprise.

I shrugged.

Cautiously she said, "I have a friend who is a ..." She paused the way one might when trying to find the words to describe a talking dog. "... he's basically a cellular biologist. Anyway, he's doing research in cell damage remediation as a curative agent for cancer. He mentioned that one of the undesirable side effects is that the treatment retards the aging process in his lab mice, complicating the study on the long-term effectiveness because the cells don't age properly."

I felt an irrational twinge of jealousy, but shoved it aside. I asked, "So you think it could be possible to travel forward in time with this treatment and not age?"

She shrugged and said, "I have no idea. It's just the only thing I can think of that might work. In a few years. Well, in a few years from 'then,' it should be well researched."

I said, "I'm afraid to chance going any further into the future beyond '46. So if there is **any** possibility of safely getting further without aging, that seems as good a risk as anything."

She nodded and asked, "Not to be morbid, but, do you think you should go into the past and fix those things before you take that chance?"

At that point, I was entirely uncertain that any good outcome was possible. I was deeply conflicted. Looking out my office window, my mind raced back to the moment that I had heard about Ellen's death. It had been such a deep cut that I had spent the next twenty years living like a hermit, working on my speculative theory to develop the technology that could take me back to undo that day. In the later years of development, as success loomed imminent, I had mentally rehearsed how I would undo my fatal mistake. It had seemed simple enough then. But everything became immeasurably more complicated when I tried it in real life.

Adding to that, the horrifying realization that Farren, my life-long best friend and research partner, had vaporized in his first time jump, compounded my quandary. And from that moment, everything I had done attempting to rescue Farren had been nothing less than disastrous.

Cautiously I replied, "I'm afraid that however I affect the past will exponentially complicate the future. And

I'm also concerned, as well as confused, about how the future events seem to have the ability to affect the past."

The psychologist in Tanya surfaced instantly. I saw it in her eyes and it made me suddenly uncomfortable. She sat on the edge of my desk and asked, "What was so urgent in the past, that you have spent all these years wanting to correct?"

I caught my breath, because I really did not want to tell her. I had never actually told the whole truth to Farren. But, there was something about her that was disarming and, hesitantly, I decided I was going to go all in.

My heart began racing as I explained, "In our senior year of high school, I ditched my date the day before our prom. She left work angry that evening, and on her way home, it was raining hard, and ... at the railroad crossing ...." My voice choked up for a few seconds. "When I saw her car afterwards, it was ... completely ripped in half .... I've desperately wanted to undo that," I finally managed to finish.

Gently touching my arm, Tanya consoled, "Survivor guilt is a natural part of grieving, especially in a traumatic event. And blaming yourself for the circumstances is also natural, but it's not healthy. There comes a point where you need to move past that assumed guilt. The first, and possibly most difficult, step is to let go of the sense of responsibility for things that were out of your control.

"And while it may seem difficult, you need to let your mind forgive yourself. Ask yourself, would this girl have wanted you to live with a lifetime of guilt?"

I tried to ignore how it felt to have Tanya's hand on my arm, but my emotions were not cooperating with my mind. With a conflicted sigh, I replied, "No, it's a lot more complicated than that. We were set up as a blind date. I'm positive that if I had handled that differently, she would probably be alive today."

"Do you regret breaking up with her?" Tanya asked. "Because if you actually can undo that kind of event with your time-phone-thing, it will undoubtedly change the trajectory of your entire life."

I was too embarrassed to explain the details surrounding that part of the situation. I just shook my head. "It wasn't like that."

"You know there's no guarantee of outcome when you're dealing with another human's mind," she cautioned.

I nodded. "I know."

Risky Venture

We discussed at length all that we knew and theorized about the anti-aging serum, and the potential hazards of forward time travel. When we had exhausted our limited knowledge and collective imaginations, we decided that the best case scenario would be to get a vial of the serum and bring it back in time. Then we could do a test injection, jump forward to the time zone in which we got the serum and, if I had not aged, then I could assume I was safe to go forward and take a vial to Farren.

It was a long shot that the serum would not mutate in the transition. In fact, the whole operation was a desperate long shot. It was unlikely that I would be able to find any of his remains. It was even less likely that his DNA was still readable.

Adding to all the uncertainty up to that point, I had the dilemma of deciding if I should inject Farren there, on Independence Day in 2276, or if I should bring the cells back in time, and inject the dead cells in our own time zone. I mused that the cells might be more likely to respond in their natural time zone. Aside from all of those concerns, there was a persistent fear that I could not shake. *What if I all of the procedures worked, and a scientific resurrection was actually possible, and I traveled "home" in time with the wrong remains? Frankenstein's monster would seem like a children's bedtime story after that.* I looked over Tanya's shoulder at the clock on the wall and thought, *It's been thirty-six hours and I've all but set the world on fire: past, present, and future.*

I had another nagging fear. I felt like we were on the verge of encroaching into God's territory of life and death. I was not sure where that line lay. But I certainly did not want to invoke Divine Wrath in the process while trying to fix my blunders. Things had been going badly enough without that.

Tanya had been watching my eyes and I suspected she was reading my mind. She asked, "Are you more afraid of the problems that lie behind, or the consequences that may yet come?"

At that moment, I was certain she was reading my mind. "I don't know," I replied meekly. I decided to not mention the concern about resurrecting the wrong person. "I have so many conflicting doubts, I'm not sure if success creates more trouble than failure, or vice versa. I'm not even sure any kind of success is possible. So far all I've done has been disastrous." I considered asking her opinion on the prospects of success, but chickened out.

I should not have worried, as she brought the question to me. "Every technological success in history has come with a price," she replied. "Do you genuinely believe the potential reward is greater than all the risk?"

I let her words soak into my brain before I answered. "I'm not entirely sure any good can come from what I've already stirred up." Then throwing emotional caution to the wind, I blurted, "Am I out of my mind? Was this whole concept of traveling back in time to change one decision a … a fool's game? Is it even possible for any good thing to come from this now?"

To my astonishment, Tanya patted my arm and gently said, "I know a girl who worked desperately hard to go to school because she wanted to change the world and fill it with love. But somewhere in time, the world changed her into a hard-bitten prison psychologist who had lost all love of life. This disaster, as you refer to it, has done her some good, I think."

Tanya's words of encouragement brought tears to my eyes. Then, in a sudden flood of memory, I recognized

her from college and I felt stricken with a fresh
lightning bolt of guilt. That did not help the tears. I tried
to formulate an apology for my partially-recalled actions
of so long in the past, but my secretary walked in at that
moment.

"Dr. Thompson?" She hesitated as her eyes darted back
and forth between Tanya, who was sitting on my desk,
and me. It was obvious from her expression that there
was no comprehension. "I, um. Sorry, I didn't see
anyone come in ..."

"Dr. Blake and I are collaborating on a project. I guess
I didn't put a note on your desk," I lamely replied. Then
realizing I was inexplicably wearing an orange prison
jumpsuit, I added, "Incognito prison research."

Judy looked blankly at me with her mouth slightly
agape. I knew if she asked one more question, I would
botch the story. She did.

"TransAmGlobFederation Penitentiary?" she asked
incredulously. Up to that point I had not even read the
label. I picked up my phone and began to key in an
escape jump, but fortunately, before I could make it
worse, Tanya intervened.

She put her hand on Judy's shoulder and flashed her
prison ID as she explained, "There's a lot of secrecy
involved in these kinds of operations, so we can't tell
you much. But Dr. Thompson has graciously, and
bravely, volunteered to infiltrate and attempt a high-risk
rescue of personnel. It's not just anyone who has the
advanced technological understanding to ferret out such
operations, and is willing to take such risks." She
paused as understanding dawned on Judy's face, then
added, "Obviously, we need you to keep this under
wraps. Exposing an undercover operative is considered
felony treason that carries a potential death penalty
with a minimum of a mandatory life sentence."

Judy nodded nervously. I felt a twinge of guilt putting
that on such a nice young lady, and at the same time I
marveled at Tanya's masterful ability to control the

situation, on the fly as it was. It occurred to me that she had never actually lied about anything either.

Still nodding, and probably somewhat in shock, Judy looked at me and indicated over her shoulder, "There's an officer here to talk to you about Dr. Helton. Um, apparently his mom turned in a missing person report." She hesitated, then asked, "Does he actually still live with his mom?"

Again Tanya took over. "He'll need to change back into his regular clothing before he speaks with the officer." She pointed to me, then to the restroom door, as she spoke. "We really can't afford to have anyone else, especially within the system, asking about our operation."

While I was changing, I heard Tanya chatting away, "Bless their hearts, but these research nerds live in their own little world which is basically ... their laboratories. They don't have much of a life, you know. You would be surprised how many of them never get out. Dates, movies, clubs, tennis, nothing. If you could stall that officer for a few minutes, that would be helpful, sweetie. Thank you so much."

I heard my office door close and reached for the doorknob. It opened from the other side, and Tanya softly said, "We've got to go now."

"You didn't knock!" I blurted in a stage whisper.

"You had plenty of time," she replied quietly. "Show me the map."

I quickly set the time and date, then held the phone, map open, for Tanya to navigate. Her brow furrowed as she muttered, "This is tougher than I thought. I think that's his lab ..."

There was a sharp rap on my office door, and I pressed the button.

What Could Possibly Go Wrong?

We landed in a public restroom with a crash. A woman who was messing with her makeup shrieked, and Tanya, in a panic, launched into action trying to calm the hysterical woman. It did not work. The woman started to hyperventilate. Frantically I went into action. I keyed in sixty seconds prior, and glanced at the door to estimate the distance. Entering an estimate of twelve feet north, I touched Tanya, and pressed the button.

We landed in the hallway outside the bathroom door exactly one minute before our prior entry, but the screaming woman was still screaming. Apparently Tanya had been touching her, so she came with us on the jump. I hit the back button and we all landed back in the bathroom. Then, yanking Tanya back away from the woman, who was on the verge of a nervous breakdown, I hit one hundred twenty seconds prior, twelve feet north.

We landed back in the hallway, miraculously both on our feet, but with Tanya leaning heavily against me for balance. The makeup lady came around the corner and nearly bumped into us on her way into the restroom. "Excuse me," she muttered irritably. "Old people making out in the hallway should be illegal." She pushed by us and through the door. It appeared she had something bothering one of her eyes.

Tanya and I looked at each other and it was all we could do to muffle our laughter.

As we headed for the office of Tanya's friend, she cautioned, "Dr. Nelson is different. Um ..." But at that instant I realized I had left the orange jumpsuit behind in the restroom in my office.

"Oh, no! The jumpsuit. It's in my office." I was rapidly trying to process a way to retrieve it without retracing all of our recent jumps.

"When we go back, we can land prior to our last arrival," Tanya replied. "Right? Isn't that what you do?"

I took a breath and explained, "I haven't been doing that in my natural time zone. I'm not sure if that negates all of the prior actions and … and I don't want to jeopardize any chance I have of rescuing Farren. I don't really know what will happen."

Looking into my eyes, she took both of my hands and, with a gentle squeeze, whispered, "We'll figure something out."

Looking at her hands in mine, I felt strangely comforted. There had been a new level of conflict brewing in the back of my mind and it surfaced at that instant. I realized that I did not want Tanya to let go of me. But I also knew the time would come, too soon, when we had to part forever.

The pause had taken too long, and when I looked back into Tanya's eyes, they were soft and welcoming. It was obvious that she had the same thoughts. Gently she extracted one of her hands and knocked on an office door. It had a placard that simply read "Dr. Nelson."

A voice bid us enter and I grudgingly released her hand as we walked into what looked like a giant mess. A young man peered at us from around a large elliptically-shaped chemical model made up of beads and sticks, suspended from the ceiling. He appeared to be assembling it. There were many such models in the room.

Tanya's words cut into my curious examination. "Dr. Nelson, this is Dr. Thompson."

The boy nodded my way and said, "Greetings, Dr. Blake. What brings you to my world?"

I was stupefied. "He's a kid!" I blurted without checking my tongue. Then in a hoarse whisper, I reworded my fear, "Is this kid supposed to help us?"

Tanya spoke aloud. "I assure you, Dr. Thompson, that Dr. Nelson is quite qualified to assist us in our quest. He is severely autistic, so his communication is a bit different than you may be accustomed to."

"What? Is he like, nineteen?" I hissed.

"Twenty-three years, eighteen weeks, two-point-seven-nine days," Dr. Nelson replied as if giving an answer to a math problem.

Tanya gave me a look that conveyed, *There, are you satisfied?*

Amazed, I asked, "When did he have time to get a Ph.D.?"

"He's got over a dozen and he's working on more," she replied, clearly enjoying my bewilderment.

"I have nineteen PhDs and four more Doctoral theses nearly ready for submission for review and defense. Prime numbers are very satisfying to me, Dr. Thompson. I prefer to keep my wall placards in prime quantities, so I submit them appropriately. The added bonus is that it disturbs the housekeeper because she cannot arrange them symmetrically. She seemingly does not have the ability to appreciate the beauty of asymmetrical assemblages." Dr. Nelson neither looked up from his model nor smiled as he spoke.

I glanced quizzically at Tanya and she explained, "He has nearly complete isolation of emotion from experience. I think it is not possible to hurt his feelings. He was a patient of mine when he was a child. His parents were understandably concerned when he expressed his disdain for normal kids' books. Then they found him reading the encyclopedia ... at the age of two. That's when they decided to seek help." She paused, then added, "We'd best get to business."

"Two," I smirked. "What took him so long?"

"I couldn't reach the shelf with the encyclopedias until then, Dr. Thompson," Dr. Nelson candidly replied. He apparently did not realize my question had been a rhetorical jest. He went on, "The idiocy that passes for children's literature is mind-numbing. It's amazing that society has not imploded."

My senses of wonder and skepticism collided. And, having no other prospects, I was about to tell him my situation, when Tanya added, "His first psychiatrist tried 'baby talk' on him. Henrik called him 'Dr. Seuss' and fired him on the spot."

I laughed aloud at the conjured image and asked, "Apparently you didn't make the same mistake?"

Shaking her head, she replied, "I asked what made him happy, and he said reading the encyclopedia. So that's what we did in our therapy sessions. We advanced to more complex reading matter after a year or so."

I had read about people like Dr. Nelson, but had never been around one. And, in those minutes of introduction, it was abundantly clear that he was capable of helping me. So I proceeded to explain my dilemma in complete detail to him. When I had finished the story, I went straight to the plea. "Dr. Blake says you have an experimental medicine that retards aging. Is there any way we could use me as a long-term experiment?"

He pondered for a moment, then replied, "Time-space specific frequencies. How brilliant. There must be a way to isolate a healthy cell's frequency, then trigger the surrounding cells to harmonically follow and thus reverse cell damage ..." He paused, then added, "You would be at a decided risk with no experimental supervision."

I waited, confused but silent. Just then, my phone beeped and I almost jumped out of my skin. "Oh my gosh! My phone is about to shut down!" I gasped in near panic. "I'm stuck here!"

Tanya looked at me like I had just grown an extra nose and, taking my phone, she slipped it into a box that looked like a miniature microwave. There was only one button and she pressed it.

My mind raced. *Is she blowing up my phone? Has she been baiting me into a trap? Am I going back to that*

psych ward? "What are you doing?" I gasped
suspiciously.

"Um, charging your phone. Hello. Are you okay?" she
retorted.

My mind calmed down to a mild roar. I sputtered, "It's
about thirty years out-of-date for any charger here.
There are bound to be drastically better batteries and
..."

A light flashed and, giving me a strange sidelong
glance, Tanya retrieved the phone. She handed it to me
and I looked at the charge indicator. It showed 100%.

I must have blinked five times before I could exclaim,
"That is ingenious! I hope the inventor got a Nobel for
that one."

Tanya pulled out her pen-shaped phone and pointed it
at the device. To my surprise, a holographic screen
popped up and she read, "Invented in 2033 by Physicist
Dr. Chadwick Thomp ..." She slowly looked over at me
and completed, "... son."

My mind reeled. "That's past my time, there must be ...
another ..." I stopped and tried to sort out thought from
emotion.

Dr. Nelson interjected, "From a purely mathematical
standpoint, you are bound to intercept your own path in
all your time jumping, as you call it."

Tanya was staring at me as if she had fallen under an
enchantment. I subconsciously took in all the peripheral
activity, but my gaze was fixed on my phone. My mind
raced to analyze the technology of a charger that could
differentiate between any device, all battery
compositions and charge capacities. Then reverse the
electron loading of the elements of the battery, while
protecting the sensitivity of the surrounding circuitry.
All without actually plugging in a jumper to redirect the
electrons.

But what really boggled me was the notion that my
first exposure to my own invention was as a consumer. I
heard my voice mutter, "I am officially freaked out right
now."

Dr. Nelson, as if nothing was amiss, said, "I accept your postulate as a project. You are correct in your assertion that you should begin with the cell-encoder serum in your natural time, then jump here. Everything, as you have noted from your research, is in a constant state of dynamic change. To make this research repeatable and viable for peer review, we need the purest data possible. So I need to get your bios now in your aged state."

"Upon your return, post injection, I will examine you for any possible side effects. We will then decide if the serum is safe enough to press further limits. It will be a challenge to sort out the effects between the two manipulators affecting you. When you jump back here, I would like you to land sixty-one seconds after you leave."

I nodded dumbly. It occurred to me later that I, the scientist who invented time travel, felt like a laboratory monkey in the presence of the savant prodigy, Dr. Nelson. It was much later when I registered the fact that his sixty-one-second timing was because it was a prime number.

The full bio workup took less than five minutes. It consisted of a finger prick to draw blood, which was analyzed on the spot, then slipped into a cryo-bag. A digital eye scan and a mouth swab completed the testing. And before I knew where to look, a full body SIM was posted on a screen with all my vital information. The depiction included my genome model.

Dr. Nelson looked at the genome image and, wielding a pencil-sized baton like a magic wand, spun it around. "Hmm," he mused, "Interesting, I had not detected that from your appearance."

I looked at Tanya, but she just shrugged. "Detected what, Dr. Nelson?" I asked nervously.

He gave me a once-over glance and replied, "Your Native American ancestry. About twenty-two percent." Then without so much as an explanation, he said, "Dr. Blake, your turn."

Tanya dutifully stepped forward, and it occurred to me that we were willing mice in the laboratory of a true mad scientist. I objected, "Dr. Blake won't be making the jump with me to the future, to the year 2276."

Absently he replied, "She is my best blind control on this experiment, Dr. Thompson. This is her natural time. When she returns, injected with the serum, she will be physically younger. It's science at its best." The young scientist was busily taking bio data from Tanya as if it was incomprehensible that she would object to being part of the experiment.

When all the data was analyzed and cataloged, Dr. Nelson gave us two, preloaded syringes. I set my app for one hour past when we jumped out and set my boss's office as our target destination. As the biochemist stepped back, he mentioned, "By the way, that needs to be intravenously administered."

Before my brain registered the final instruction, my finger hit the button. We landed hard, but on our feet, and at that instant I realized there needed to be an elevation sensor added to my program. *It's like we're hitting the floor the way a person does when there is one less step than anticipated when going down stairs. That explains the sore knees,* I thought.

The Best-Laid Plans

Phillip jumped up from his desk, overturning his chair. "My gosh! What are you doing here?" he gasped.

"What are you doing here?" I retorted irritably.

"You brought us to an occupied office?" Tanya blurted incredulously.

"He's never here when I need him," I snapped.

Phillip demanded, "Who's she? The cops are looking for you! What have you done with Farren? Why are you in my office?"

"Long story, long story, I know. Are they out of my office yet?" I replied in a swirl of panic.

"The place is crawling with them! They've called in the FBI and I heard someone say this is a CIA matter! Do you know how serious this is? And how did you just vanish for an hour?" Phillip's face was practically glowing red as he excitedly whispered.

"You don't know the half!" I countered a bit too rudely. "I need a phone charger. Can I borrow yours? You can get mine off my desk. And ... we need you to call the nurse up here. There's a ..."

"Did she just take drugs?" Phillip interrupted, suddenly turning very pale.

As I tried to explain, Tanya pulled my sleeve up and slapped my arm to get a vein to show. It was not difficult, as my blood pressure was probably setting a world record. "It's a ... medicine, we're part of an experiment ..."

Phillip's eyes rolled back and he fainted. Tanya inserted the needle into my vein and I felt a strange flush throughout my body and tasted metal. I looked at

Tanya with a new amazement. She shrugged and said, "I
put myself through grad school working as a
phlebotomist."

I hastily stood Phillip's chair upright as Tanya helped
him up and into it. He was clearly in shock. By the
commotion outside his office door, I knew we were about
to have a visitation. I grabbed the phone charger and,
having already preset our return to Dr. Nelson's office, I
said, "Grab the needles."

Tanya was ahead of me. She held them up like she was
about to share lollipops, and wrapped her arm around
my waist. The door smashed open and I heard the
distinct crackle of multiple TASERs being fired. I braced
myself for the burn, but felt the floor of Dr. Nelson's
office instead. Tanya had her hand on my phone when I
looked down. "You're welcome," she said.

"Was Phillip directly behind us when we jumped?" I
asked.

Tanya grimaced, "Oh! Oh, that's not good."

I just shook my head empathetically, "Sorry, Phillip …
sorry," was all I could say.

"Remarkable," Dr. Nelson said. "Tanya, you will need
some clothing that fits before you launch into the future.
I wonder if the weight loss is directly attributable to the
age, or if it too is subject to a signature frequency."

I almost choked in surprise at his impropriety, but
Tanya just laughed. "Dr. Nelson, age and weight are two
subjects that are typically taboo with women. But I
understand that you are processing data. You just might
not want to broach those subjects with most women."

With knitted brow, Dr. Nelson nodded, "I see." It was
apparent that he did not. Then he pressed a button to
summon his secretary.

In seconds, the eyelash lady from our bathroom
experience walked in. I braced myself, but she
apparently did not recognize us thirty-odd years
younger. Cynically I thought, *I should kiss Tanya now,
and see if Eyelash thinks it's okay for young people to
make out in public.* But my reverie was interrupted by

Dr. Nelson's statement, "Marsha, my friend Tanya here needs clothing that fits. She's a bit slimmer than you, and she needs to be dressed more practically for the field experiment I'm sending her on. So, take her to the mailroom, ask for Miss Carson, and instruct Miss Carson to outfit Tanya with street clothing. Thank you."

As she left with Tanya, Marsha sucked in and stretched taller as if that would change reality. And as the door clicked closed, I could no longer contain my mirth. I burst into laughter and explained his gaff to Dr. Nelson. But he just gave me a quizzical look and said, "But I ended with a thank you."

I decided anyone working with a genius of his level needed to understand his handicap as well as his genius. Curiosity got me at that point and I asked, "How do you know the lady in the mailroom is the same size as Tanya?"

"I see her when I pick up my mail. She wears a different outfit each day and rotates on a ten day wardrobe, although she has twenty-nine potential combinations. She also maintains two employee lockers, which indicates she is self-conscious and keeps at least one extra outfit at work." Dr. Nelson was taking my bios as he spoke.

"How do you remember all that stuff?" I muttered rhetorically.

He paused and, with a dismissive shrug, replied, "I remember everything, Dr. Thompson. I remember the rhythm of my mother's heartbeat when she was in labor with me. I've been told by numerous experts, that is not normal."

I was too stunned to ask any further questions.

When Tanya returned, she looked amazing, but was clearly bothered by something. I did not have to ask, as she blurted right out, "Dusty pink. Not my color."

"The fit is perfect," Dr. Nelson suggested.

"The fit is perfect," she agreed, "but the color and style are not me."

"I think you look good," I interjected without thinking.

"Color is merely a light frequency. Dr. Thompson can change that for you when you time jump," Dr. Nelson said as if it would be a simple programming feat.

Suddenly I came to my senses and, perhaps too forcefully, snapped, "Oh, no! No! No one is time jumping with me two centuries into the future!" I regained control of my emotions and more calmly added, "It's too dangerous. I've got to do this alone."

Eyelash Marsha gasped and backed out the door. Tanya gave me one of those looks that expressed, *Smooth move*. Dr. Nelson countered, "We need an observer in the event that you die or there is some other side effect from the serum. It may affect people unequally. This is important research."

I pointed at the device charger and stated, "That will disappear the instant I die. You'll know. Albeit, you can't tell anyone. But no one else needs to die with me. This whole mess is ... it's my fault."

"It's settled then," Dr. Nelson said as he pulled a syringe from a chilled cabinet, "I'll go with."

"NO!" Tanya and I blurted simultaneously. Then before I could say any more, Tanya added, "I'm going." She held up my phone triumphantly. I had not noticed that she had taken it from the charger oven. She continued with a flash of passion in her eyes, "At this point, my life here is a chaotic disaster. If you don't return ... if you die, I lose everything. I'll end up in the psych unit where I worked, and I would sooner die in the uncharted void of time." She then looked into my eyes and calmly stated, "I'm not leaving your side until history demands it."

"Listen," I urged, "I can drop you back in your office at a time before I was sentenced to the ward. No one could possibly associate you with me at that point. This is entirely too dangerous! The, the risk of death by unimaginable sources is ... is probably ... inevitable."

It occurred to me at that moment that I was going to die in the same place that Farren had. Dr. Nelson watched us argue back and forth like a judge, and I

wondered if he was going to stand us in corners for a
timeout.

"My fate is inextricably tied to yours at this point," she
retorted. "If you never return, and everything
miraculously turns out okay here, now, then I am stuck
with a hopeless sense of what could have been. I've
already wasted most my life building a career I detest,
and not actually living."

"Your work isn't meaningless," I lamely pointed out,
knowing she was correct. I understood exactly how she
felt, and I also recognized the fact that she had,
chronologically, thirty-two years more of it than I had.

Tanya smirked and mockingly added, "Besides, imagine
my secretary, passing my doorway and, presto, there I
am, thirty-some years younger. 'Are you Dr. Blake's
daughter?' 'No, I'm still me. I just slipped out for a spa
break. I recommend the cucumber and mud bath, it'll
erase three decades in a nanosecond or two.' "

I was stupefied, but before I could think of a single
word to reply, Dr. Nelson said, "I don't understand."

It took me a few seconds to register the novelty of that
statement, but the look of disbelief on Tanya's face
spoke volumes. Tanya's question came out as an amazed
statement. "I've known you since you were two and I
have never heard those words from your mouth."

"How do you people do it? You meet, and interact, and
just bond. It's like magic. Then you selflessly defend the
welfare of one another, even to the point of internal
conflict. Ultimately, you marry and have offspring. It's a
mystery that is unexplainable by science." Dr. Nelson's
muse was genuine.

I was about to explain that we were not an item, but
Tanya, ever the student of the human psyche, read
through the unspoken part of his muse and replied, "It's
not so difficult as it may appear. She likes retro fashion
and natural color coordination. She has a two-year-old
daughter. Her late husband died in a construction
accident just before the baby was born. That's when she
started working here. She likes chocolate-flavored

coffee, cuddly little animals, and, oddly enough, mountain biking. My quick assessment is that she is about 135 IQ points below you, so she doesn't understand a word you say. But she has a heart of gold. Buy her a chocolate cappuccino. Sit down and listen to her, don't discuss any research, don't give her any advice, and don't look at a clock."

When Tanya finished her matchmaking lesson, Dr. Nelson just nodded. I half expected him to write notes, but then remembered that he had complete recall. I was also acutely aware that Tanya had gotten very close to me.

Dr. Nelson looked down at his desk and began to theorize, "I wonder if there is some radio-transmittable signal attached to endorphins that signal and receive from mutually attracted individuals? A love resonance, of sorts. There must be a quantifiable scientific metric that has yet to be identified. Like a sixth sense. But if it signals to the amygdala, it could be undetectable by people like myself."

He looked up at us and, at that moment, I was grateful that I did not live inside Dr. Nelson's mind. Tanya replied softly, "Dr. Nelson, this situation is sort of urgent."

Then without missing a beat, he looked at me and remarked, "I've given some thought to your quest. By my calculations, your friend's remains are two hundred-nineteen years beyond their statistically natural life span. And given the climate of the region in which they are interred, and calculating the trajectory of change within that climate, and allowing for a ten percent factor of unknown vectors, your friend's remains should contain a small amount of readable DNA. But it should be a sufficient quantity provided he has not been burned."

I blinked and nodded, which Dr. Nelson must have taken for concurrence. He continued, "But, there is a great risk if you resuscitate him that far into the future, that his DNA-frequency encoding will jump time, so to speak, and become natural to that zone. Eventually, my serum will wear off, and in his organic time he may simply cease to exist. I think that would be a bad thing."

Dr. Nelson was clearly expecting me to weigh in on the analysis, but I was still trying to process how he could comprehend my life's worth of research in less than an hour of lapsed chronological time. He apparently grew impatient and added, "You could add a feature to your device's program that would infinitely adjust his DNA so that it always recognized the current time zone and believes it belonged there. To a limited sense, that is an undesirable side effect that my serum is accomplishing."

I discovered that I was nodding dumbly as Dr. Nelson spoke. Finally I collected my senses and responded, "Once I get everything reset to the place it was before I started messing up history, I plan to destroy the devices and all the research documents. So, in answer to your idea, no, I'll not be updating the software. There's just too much risk involved."

He gave me a curious look and replied, "You must realize that you can't be the only person in history who has unlocked the secrets of time manipulation ... right? Ponder the probabilities for a second." He paused to let that sink in and added, "Even if you are the first, undoubtedly there are others out there in the future, maybe even the distant future, who have developed a method of time travel."

His use of the past tense verb describing future events twisted my sense of linear propriety.

Interrupting, Tanya muttered, "You guys are hurting my brain."

That struck me as ironic coming from the woman who, literally minutes earlier, had peered into the minds of two people and exposed their suppressed inner longings for love and companionship, and then formulated advice for them, all in under five minutes.

"Do I look that silly in this outfit?" Tanya asked me. I looked up from my reverie and realized I had been gazing at her.

I blushed uncontrollably and, before my brain filtered my words, I blurted, "You look pretty hot." Then I really blushed and, trying to recover my verbal blunder, continued with, "I mean, well, what I intended was ..."

Cutting me off, Tanya took my arm and said, "Let's go rescue Farren." I had the distinct sense that she was saving me from myself. Before I could say anything else, she handed me my phone.

I opened it and verbally checked off, "Battery – 100%. Location - Independence Hall, intersection of Market and Independence Mall, North 39.950627, West 75.148908. Time ... I've been thinking I should land two hours after Farren, so I can tap into eye witness reports to find his remains. Does that make sense?"

Tanya gave me a funny look and said, "You're the time lord here, lead on."

At the same time, Dr. Nelson nodded assent. "That seems the most logical for a blind jump."

"Time – 2 PM, July 4th, 2276." I finished my prejump check list. Then to Tanya, who had my left arm securely wrapped with her arms, I asked, "Are you really sure you want to do this?"

"I can't think of anywhere else I would rather die," she replied.

Perplexed, I asked, "Twenty-two seventy-six?"

Her eyes rolled and she replied, "That's a time, not a place."

"Independence Hall?" I queried.

"In your arms. Wow. Come on time jumper, let's make this date memorable," was her exasperated response.

Before I even processed her words, I heard Dr. Nelson comment, "You two are remarkably romantic."

I pressed the button.

Dichotomy

It is not every day a person gets to jump so far out of their time that absolutely nothing is familiar. As the sensation of our feet touching ground resonated into my mind, I realized I may not even be able to communicate with the people of that century. Oddly enough, the immigration of my great-grandparents into the United States came to mind. But I did not have a lot of time to ponder it because I was too stunned by what I saw.

Tanya spoke first. "This is exactly not what I was expecting," she whispered.

I was suddenly very aware that she had not released my arm. "It's so tranquil," I whispered in reply.

We were in a small meadow that I estimated to be about forty acres. The surrounding forest was mature with a random mix of hardwoods and firs that could only be natural. The sounds of birds flitting about and chattering in the lush forest seemed too serene to interrupt, and in the distance I could hear a gentle stream trickling over rocks. Some small creature was startled by our sudden appearance and scurried into a crevice in the moss-covered rock outcrop we had landed beside. A small flock of birds erupted from the forest to our right and, flying across the meadow, found a more suitable tree to land in on the opposite side. The breeze wafted the sweet smell of old decaying leaves blended with that of fresh vegetation. All of my senses told me that the forest was comfortably over a hundred years old.

While my senses were filled with the pureness of the place, my mind flashed through the possibilities. *Did*

*they finally accomplish peace on earth? Was there a
holocaust that scrubbed humans from the planet? Have
they made cities into greenscapes? Did I transpose
coordinates?* The possibilities mounted rapidly as my
mind whirled.

Tanya whispered the question I had not considered.
"Did we go the wrong direction in time?"

I almost choked on my obvious oversight and pulled up
my phone for a quick check. The review showed that we
were, in fact, in the year 2276 AD. I checked the other
factors and verified that we were also at the correct
coordinates. "I don't understand what's happened here,"
I muttered in confusion.

Tanya gently put her head against my chest and
whispered, "Your heart is racing."

I had the strong urge to kiss her, but the imminent
reality of our ultimate separation restrained me. I felt
like I had complicated enough situations and that I did
not need to add that to the list. Foolishly I said, "I'm
going to miss you when it comes time for us to part."

Without lifting her head she replied, "My mother used
to say, 'Worrying about the future is like going to the
doctor before you are injured.' It sounds better in
Japanese."

We stood there in the serenity for several long minutes,
and I had a lucid fantasy of building a little cabin in that
clearing and starting life over with Tanya in that time
and place. But my "Little House on the Prairie" reverie
was crashed by the reality that the serum would wear
off and it would all end abruptly and too soon.

A subconscious nudge in the periphery of my memory
reminded me that we were there with a purpose. "We
should find Farren," I whispered.

"I think he's right there," Tanya stated with disarming
nonchalance as she pointed to an area where the grass
was beaten down.

"Is it that easy?" I asked aloud.

I felt her head nod and she murmured, "I wish we
didn't have to leave."

"Me too," I whispered. "I really don't want this moment to end." Then before I could say anything stupid, she released me and gingerly stepped toward the disturbed area of grass.

It was heavily trampled and a central spot had been cleared to the dirt. It was about the size of a human. But the detail that captivated me was that there were a lot of boot tracks. "We're not alone here after all," I said with disappointment.

Tanya had taken a few steps to follow a trail that was beaten into the grass when she paused and called back to me, "There appears to be a path over here."

I had an eerie premonition that something was amiss. As I hurried to catch up to her, a gunshot rang out with deafening nearness. I jumped and Tanya jumped more so. As she landed, she turned and all but fell into my arms. My mind whirled, and I blurted, "I expected them to have ray guns by now!"

But she did not respond. Her eyes rolled back in a faint. And I barely kept her from falling to the ground as she slumped into my arms.

The sensation of warm sticky fluid flowing freely down my arm and dripping from my fingertips electrified me with horror. "This can't be!" I gasped aloud.

In a fog of confusion, I lowered Tanya to the ground. I was soaked with blood from the wound in her chest. And I could not bring myself to examine the exit wound on her back. I knew it had to be large.

Everything seemed to stop in my mind. I heard many more gunshots and a voice kept crying out, "NO! NO! NO!" I finally realized that was me and managed to stop speaking, but could not control my sobbing.

In minutes, we were surrounded by a rabble army, and I wondered if they were a local militia or some sort of a guerrilla rebel force. Nothing made sense. One of the soldiers, a man with stark white skin and red hair that swirled out from under a green beret, grabbed me by the shoulder and urged, "Let's go, brother! They'll be back any minute!"

"Why did they kill my girlfriend?" I heard my voice demand with startling clarity.

"Buddy, we killed that she-devil. **They're** trying to kill you," Red replied. Then seeing my baffled, and undoubtedly shocked, expression, he shook his head and called out to his men, "We've got another planter. Let's get him to the compound for deprogramming."

Then to me, Red spoke as if I were a child, "You've been programmed. Drugged and brainwashed, to believe all their lies. They're tryin' to wipe out our bloodlines and take over our territory. But it ain't happening on my watch."

"Whaaat?" I blurted.

Red slapped my shoulder and explained, "You'll be better in a few days. Takes a while for the drugs to wear off."

My mind exploded in panic and I exclaimed, "My friend, my girlfriend, has been murdered!"

Red shook me by the shoulder and snapped, "That woman wasn't no friend of yours. She's one of them. They do that. Get your mind in their control, so they can get to us. But it's always a trap."

"Who are you talking about?" I shouted. My head was swimming from his illogical babbling.

"The blacks! They've been trying to take our land for a long time! But we've got deep roots here. And we'll never surrender our homeland." Red was pretty worked up, and my mind was in a muddle.

I've landed into the middle of a white supremacist compound! It's like a redneck trailer park joke, only nothing is amusing and Tanya is dead! I thought in panic. *My phone! I've got to take us back! Ten minutes. Maybe twenty.* I reached for my phone, but just then someone called out, "Blacks!"

Automatic gunfire erupted from two directions and Red's white militia returned fire. I was deafened and dropped to the ground over Tanya's body. Somewhere in the chaos, I had the odd thought, *I wonder if this will bother Tanya's hearing when I get her back in time to come back to life.* It made no sense, but I covered her ears just in case.

The attack was apparently repelled and Red pulled me up. "Let's go, brother! We'll get your head back on straight in a few days." And he all but dragged me toward the tree line.

"Wait!" I called out hotly, "I'm not leaving without my friend!"

Red took me by both shoulders and bluntly stated, "She ain't your friend! She's an enemy combatant! And she's dead! You'll thank me later. Let's go!"

There was another sudden burst of gunfire and the white militia launched into action again. I took my opportunity and ran toward Tanya's body. I was no more than a dozen steps away when a bullet tore through my shoulder and another hit me in the thigh. Somehow in the pain and pandemonium, I never lost consciousness as I crawled the last few feet to Tanya. My hand touched her face and, at that moment, a new sound erupted. I heard someone yell, "Missionaries!" And I realized the militia was retreating. A sound like a high voltage electric arc was snapping violently, and I knew if I did not hurry, I was about to see my first, and probably last, ray gun.

I pulled out my phone and laboriously opened it. I made sure to make skin contact with Tanya and pressed return. Nothing happened. I looked through blurry eyes at the screen. Battery – 1%, it read. "Oh, no! Battery life is spent proportionally to the amount of time jumped!" I exclaimed aloud. "I should have thought of that!"

I realized that I was well on my way to bleeding to death, and I remembered Tanya's words. I pulled myself closer and kissed her forehead. "I'm so sorry," I half-whispered and half-cried. Suddenly a shadow loomed over me, and I rolled over and saw what could have passed for a poor imitation of a Star Wars stormtrooper.

He was pointing some kind of weapon at me and I kicked his leg. He stumbled slightly and shot me. The arc I had heard turned out to be a highly-advanced cordless TASER-like weapon being fired. It felt as if my entire nervous system had been injected with acid. My voluntary muscles were instantly and completely sabotaged.

Several people arrived and someone pulled out what looked like a remote. He pointed it at me and, to my astonishment, the pain disappeared, other than the probes stuck into my skin. Yet I was held completely incapable of movement. It was brilliant in design.

The guy with the remote began moving his thumb and, beyond all my imagination, and completely outside my will, I stood up and walked to the awaiting transport. I lay down on a stretcher, which looked surprisingly the same as they did from my time. I tried to call out in protest as they zipped Tanya into a body bag, but I was unable to speak because of the restraining probe. I watched helplessly as they loaded her into a separate transport.

As the transport began to move, I wondered if they were on wheels or were floating. The first bone-jarring hole we hit answered that question.

My mind raced as they performed a miraculous healing of my bullet wounds. A device that looked like a hair dryer was aimed at the wound, and it healed before my eyes. I could actually feel my shoulder blade heal inside. The procedure was repeated on the thigh wound with the same results. I wanted to ask so many questions, but could not. For a moment, I hoped they were treating Tanya to the same medical level, but knew that would

not be the case. I closed my eyes and must have passed
out.

Mission Hospital

My eyes opened with a start, and I found myself in near total darkness. Instinctively I asked, "What was the deal with that TASER?"

A soft voice responded, "The TASER was invented by Jack Cover in 1969. It has undergone numerous advancements through the centuries. The latest upgrade was the walking control by Thomas Swift in 2252. It is considered, by law enforcement, to be an outmoded weapon."

"Who are you? Where am I?" I asked in confusion.

The voice answered, "You are in Bed 328 of the New England Penitentiary Missionary Hospital. There are no other beings in the room with you, so your first question is invalid."

"Who are you?" I asked again, feeling rather creeped out.

The voice responded, "There are no other beings in the room with you, so your question is invalid."

"Where is Tanya?" I almost cried when I said her name.

"The question is too broad. Please clarify with more details," was the response.

I pondered my plight and it did not look good. I was completely disoriented, strapped to a bed, talking to some invisible machine, and I knew not where my phone was. I decided to pick the machine's brain, figuratively. "How do I address you?"

"There are no other beings in the room with you, so your question is invalid." I was really getting sick of that response.

"What are your valid commands?" I tried, speaking directly at what I assumed was the device. In the darkness, with only a few soft lights to give any definition, it looked rather like a standing lamp.

"There is no command code on any MDI device that is available to an inmate or undocumented personnel," the machine replied.

"Do you have a reference number? Is there a list of valid questions?" I asked.

The lamp replied, "My identification code is MDI-328-CMH. All recognized questions in this vicinity will be answered using Direct-Link filtration. A request preceded by 'MDI dash 328 dash CMH,' or the authorized abbreviation, '328,' will be answered directly by this unit."

"Wow. You're quite the chatty droid," I said, and was not surprised that 328 did not respond. *Okay,* I thought, *this thing is really a giant internet sourcing device, or search engine, maybe like Siri, but on steroids. Now, how do I get this thing to help me get my phone and find a power source?* I asked, "328, why am I tethered to this bed?"

"You are not tethered," the device answered.

"What is wrapped around my arm?" I asked.

328 replied, "A MW-SL probe is temporarily attached to your arm for medical observation and security. The wrap is to protect the probe from snagging on other objects. Upon being chipped for permanent monitoring, the MW-SL will be removed."

I phrased my next question carefully. "Am I free to move around the hospital, unaccompanied?"

"Yes, you may move about freely. This MDI unit will remain within 3.5 meters of the MW-SL probe for transmission efficiency," 328 answered.

I had expected that to be the case. I also knew there would be some alarm if I broke any of the rules. I just did not know what those rules were.

"What do they do with corpses here?" I asked.

"Deceased inmates are kept in the morgue and, if no family collects the remains within 24 hours, they are incinerated, in compliance with all applicable UC inmate interment codes," 328 replied.

My mind reeled with one thought: *Twenty-four hours!* Urgently I asked, "How long have I been in here? What is the date and time?"

"Today is July 5, 2276. The time is 5:05 am. You have been registered in this facility for fourteen hours and twenty-seven minutes."

"Am I considered an inmate? Is there human staff at the hospital? Or is there a list of permissible activities for me?" I asked.

328 responded, "All occupants of New England are classified as inmates. Your official classification is: Undocumented, Unlabeled, Third generation, Wild born, Penn Region 12, Unknown affiliation. The New England Penitentiary Missionary Hospital staff has 554 registered volunteers and paid staff that includes 29 physicians, 94 intern physicians, 12 chaplains, 75 RNs, 233 nurse interns, 9 administrators, and 102 support staff."

"How is Pennsylvania considered to be part of New England? And what is New England Penitentiary?" I asked with some uncertainty.

As 328 began to answer, a light came on, and a tall woman in her mid-fifties walked in. "That will do, 328," she said as she approached my bed.

"MDI-328-CMH is standing by to report, playback, or retrieve any data required for Administrator Bergman," my talking lamp responded.

I almost felt jealous. I thought, *328 responds to Bergman's commands.* I said, "Dr. Bergman, there's been a huge error here. I am considered an inmate, but I have not committed a crime. I stumbled into some kind of racial war and was nearly killed in the process."

Bergman watched me silently as I made my plea, so I continued, "My friend ... girlfriend, was murdered before my eyes. I really need your help getting out of here."

"My title is Administrator Bergman, not Doctor," the woman replied cordially. "Your request is, of course, ridiculous. Perhaps your injuries damaged your memory. Let's begin with a name, date of birth, and home region. Do you remember any of those details?"

I considered making up a name, but dismissed the idea instantly. "I'm Chad Thompson from North Carolina," I answered. I conveniently skipped my birthdate and again asserted, "There really has been a mix up, and I am not supposed to be here."

Bergman listened patiently, but furrowed her brow. "Much of your story is impossible, Mr. Thompson. You are neither chipped, tattooed, nor tagged, which leaves only one other possibility. You had to be born here in the penitentiary." The administrator seemed to have only one calm emotion. "Were your parents convicts?"

"No," I replied.

Bergman wrote on a tablet and asked, "Are you affiliated with any organization, gang, or movement?"

"No," I repeated.

She recorded that then asked again, "Place of birth?"

I decided to try a new tack. "I am confused about everything. I feel like I've been dropped off from another planet or something. Would you please explain to me what this is all about?"

Bergman regarded me a long time before she spoke. "To answer your question to 328, Pennsylvania is part of the one-half million square kilometer reserve set aside by the United Council after the war of 2149. The local level of anarchy was determined to be greater than 85%, or some such amount, whatever the minimum level was supposed to be back then. The region was walled in and no outside commerce has been allowed. It was labeled the New England Penitentiary, and has served as the world's prison since then. It is, if you will excuse the indignity of it, a human dumping ground.

"There has been no law or order within the penitentiary for over a century, and warlords have ruled most of the region since. Some districts are ruthlessly violent, beyond comprehension. There once stood a great, proud city right here. It's all gone now. I have seen old documents of the city. It was beautiful, but overgrown rubble is all that remains. Lawlessness will do that for you, Mr. Thompson. In the Church, we refer to that as unchecked sin. Destruction, deception, and darkness are the fruit of such sin."

328 interrupted, "Cleaning staff entering the room."

The administrator ignored the machine and the cleaning lady, who went dutifully to work. Bergman continued, "When the population of New England hit its apogee in the thirties, the United Council ruled that the military could use the inmates for live-fire training. That practice continues still. That is something we, the Church, find reprehensible and strongly condemn. Our estimate is that at least 55% of the inmates in New England were born here as third generation or greater.

"That is where you are in this mess, Mr. Thompson. Since you are not marked by any of the regular entry labels, you had to be wildborn in New England. Yet you insist that you came from a foreign country and are here by mistake. That's not possible. So, why do you remain uncooperative? We are the Church, not some warlord. We exist to bring relief to the suffering and light of the Gospel into a world of darkness. You can be honest here, Mr. Thompson."

I was stunned by the whole concept. I asked, "How do inmates have automatic weapons? And who were the stormtroopers in white armor?"

She was watching my eyes as I spoke, and I could not figure out why she was so concerned about my identity and origin. Bergman answered gingerly, "The white armor is simply bullet resistant gear that the mission's security forces wear. The UC allows us to serve in here with certain restrictions. We employ non-lethal weapons to protect the hospital and staff, and even the victims of the violence in which they have participated. Most warlords honor our mission to help, but some are entirely vicious and must be restrained so we can minister healing to those in need, as we can."

Ms. Bergman looked at me for a long moment before she continued. "A warlord-run society will inevitably result in war and destruction. But their antiquated technology can only produce weapons that are long obsolete. From our perspective, those weapons of a bygone era are of little consequence to a properly shielded facility and staff."

Again Administrator Bergman paused, then, before she spoke again, she pulled my phone from her pocket. Holding it up she said, "Your interest in the weapons of the warlords is of great concern to me. This was found in your possession and, though it is an obvious antique, it is constructed of extremely complex circuitry." She looked at me and demanded, "Mr. Thompson, look me in the eye and tell me the whole truth. What is this? Is it a weapon of mass destruction? Is it a technology-siphoning device? What is this thing, and why did you have it? And how did it get inside the penitentiary?"

"If there are no laws here, why do you care?" I challenged.

"Sir, I am responsible for the welfare of hundreds of volunteers and staff. If this device is a potential threat to their well being, I have to take such things seriously," she urged.

Okay lady, you asked for it, I thought. I took a deep breath and said, "It's my cell phone. I invented a way to travel in time, and that's how I got here. I need ... I demand that you return my phone to me. And I must insist that you take me to Tanya, my ... companion, who was killed in the firefight back at, what used to be, Independence Hall."

"So you just dropped in from some time in the future?" Bergman asked incredulously.

I shook my head. "The past," I replied matter-of-factly. "More than 200 years in the past."

The administrator erupted in laughter, and I was not sure if I had victoriously found her second emotion, or just condemned myself to another psychiatric vacation.

"I can prove it to you, Administrator Bergman. Let me have my phone, please," I insisted.

To my astonishment, she asked, "Why are you taking anti-cancer medication, since your scans revealed no trace of cancer? And how did you come by such treatment inside the penitentiary?"

I was stupefied. "It's an experimental medication that I am using to not age during time travel," I told her.

She instantly came back with, "What is this device? They are of great concern to us here."

In a flash I realized it. "You have Farren's phone too! Are his remains here?"

Her eyes narrowed and, before she could speak, I went on the offensive. "Give me both phones, and take me to the remains of Farren and Tanya, and we will all disappear and your problems will vanish."

"How many of you are there?" she asked suspiciously.

I held up my hand with three fingers up. "Three people, two phones, poof, we'll be gone. And … there is some chance we can affect the past to make your world get miraculously better."

"Uh-huh," she remarked sarcastically. "Suddenly better."

Good, I thought, *we've found another emotion*. "You don't believe God can use things like this to accomplish miracles? You do believe in miracles? Right?" I knew I sounded desperate.

"Humph," she retorted, and with that she turned briskly and, nearly bowling the cleaning lady over, marched from the room.

I turned to the lamp and asked, "328, can we follow her to her office?"

"According to UC Code 2199.03.12.MVNPS.15.919, Stalking a Staff or Volunteer at a Mission-run Relief Facility is a Class 1 crime, which carries a potential sentence of death," 328 responded.

"How did the world get so messed up?" I asked rhetorically.

There was no reply.

In agitation, I gave the MDI unit a scowl and asked, "Well, 328, how did the world get this messed up?"

The response was, "Your question is too broad. Please clarify with more details."

For the first time, I felt completely lost. My despair simmered into a rage, and I contemplated fighting my way into Bergman's office to get my phone. But then I remembered that it was completely dead. I had a second low of despair.

"Señor, I believe in miracles," a Hispanic-sounding voice said softly.

I looked over my shoulder at the cleaning lady and almost fell over. Beyond all my expectations, she was holding up not only my phone, but Farren's as well. "How did you get those?" I blurted.

The older woman flashed a grin that included about half of the normal allotment of teeth. "Boss Lady almost spilled them into my hands when she ran over me. Just then the angel said to me, 'Look, there is your miracle.' So I took the boxes for you."

"You're a saint," I whispered.

"No, señor. I was sentenced here as a pickpocket," came the toothless reply.

"Can you tell me how to get to the morgue?" I asked.

Again the old woman smiled and replied, "That is my next room to clean. I can take you there."

The Maintenance Room

I asked the cleaning lady, "How long are you sentenced to New England Penitentiary?"

The woman gave me an odd look and replied, "There is only one sentence here, señor. It is until you die."

I was less shocked than incensed. "For pickpocketing?"

"In Tijuana, my home city, there is no tolerance for anyone unless they are connected to a gang that pays the government. And there is no mercy. Especially if you try to steal something back from them," the old woman replied as she finished up her chores.

"You were convicted of stealing because you took something back that belonged to you?" I asked to clarify my indignation.

She shrugged and answered, "I should have stayed closer to my brother. They do not 'tax' people like him on the street."

"How long have you been here? In the penitentiary, I mean?" I asked.

"Fourteen years, señor. And twelve here working for the hospital," she replied.

"Do they pay you here?" I asked.

She scowled suspiciously and shook her head to the negative. I wondered what kind of arrangement could possibly be agreeable to someone to work for free. She answered my unasked question. "The food here is very good and every hour in the hospital is safer than the war outside."

They should pay their help anyway, I thought to myself, but did not press the issue. My next urgent item of business was how to charge my phone. Since its technology was two and a half centuries old, I assumed I would have to improvise a solution. The charger that I had taken from Phillip's office was gone. No doubt it was in Bergman's office. I had an idea, but did not want to set off any of 328's alarms.

"328, how is electricity generated and processed in this century?" I asked, hoping it would seem innocuous enough.

There was a nearly imperceptible whir as 328 came back online. "An estimated 78% of the energy consumed on the planet is generated by hybrid regenerative solar/radon fuel cells, 20% is generated in geothermal/crystal-distortion mines, and the remaining 2% is generated by various primitive methods of carbon-based fuel combustion. The civilized world has an extensive power grid network, and current is transmitted on 333 volt alternating current at 20,000 hertz."

"Twenty thousand hertz," I muttered in exasperation. "How in the world am I going to tame that frequency?"

There was no answer. It occurred to me that if there was a person present, 328 would not answer unless it was directly addressed. I glanced at the cleaning lady, who was watching me like she expected something special. "What is your name?" I asked, then hastily rephrased it into Spanish, "Como se llama?"

The cleaning lady's face lit up and she replied, "Maria Adriana Garcia-Fernandez." Then she excitedly launched into a Spanish monologue that I did not understand.

"Maria," I motioned to slow the verbal tide, "I don't have that much Spanish ... no hablo Espanol!"

She nodded and gave me a knowing smile for the effort. I asked "Are there any device-charging ... devices here in the hospital?"

Shrugging, Maria said, "I do not understand what you are asking."

Deftly I removed the battery from my phone and read the information. I almost asked 328 if there was a device to charge the 2680 milliamp lithium-ion battery, but had a moment of panic. "328, do you record all video and audio in the room?"

"MDI units are equipped to record and play back all audio and any attached inputs from medical accessories. No MDI unit is equipped with video capability," was the reply.

I chickened out on my charger question and cryptically motioned for Maria to look at the battery. "Do you know how to recharge this?" I asked, hoping that would not be too much information for whomever might be eavesdropping.

Maria shook her head with a look of confusion that confused me. *How in the world do they charge their stuff these days?* I mused irritably to myself.

I looked around for a rechargeable device, forgetting entirely about 328. I finally noticed a small protrusion under the skin behind Maria's ear. *That would be her tracking chip,* I assumed. "How do they recharge that?" I asked, pointing, but got the same confused shrug.

I'm going to have to hotwire a transformer, I thought. "328, is there a maintenance shop in the hospital?"

My talking lamp responded, "The Maintenance Department is located in the west wing of Level 1."

Looking at Maria, I nodded and said, "I'll meet you in the morgue in a half hour to forty-five minutes." Then to 328, I asked, "328, how do I get from here to Level 1 and the west wing?"

As my talking robot gave me turn-by-turn instructions along the way to the maintenance shop, I tried to calculate how much time I could expect before Bergman discovered that the phones were gone. I knew she could locate me instantly as long as I was within range of 328. I had also presumed that if I tried to get away from 328, it would probably sound an alarm.

I messed with the probe in my arm enough to learn that it was barbed. I cringed at the thought of ripping it out of my skin. That complicated my escape plan, such that it was. I had come to suspect that anything in significant contact with me, when I time jumped, would come with. But items making only casual contact did not have the same effect except with humans skin-to-skin. I was beginning to theorize that there was an electromagnetic impulse harmonization between two objects that are closely associated, similar to a gravitational attraction. My mind wandered down that trail, wondering where the fine line of disassociation was within the electronic scanners of my machine. I also pondered how I could manipulate that logarithmic identifier to leave behind items at my discretion.

What am I thinking? I thought. *I have to destroy this technology as soon as I can unwind all the time bombs I have wound up! Why am I even pondering the next evolution of this thing?*

The instructions from 328 had stopped, and I suddenly became aware that we were standing in front of a door. Looking up, I saw the sign. Property Maintenance, it read. I reached for the doorknob and, as I turned it, someone shouted, "Hey! You! Where do you think you're going?"

My pulse skyrocketed and I darted through the doorway with 328 on my heels. A quick glance around revealed ample hiding places for me, but my escort was not quite as flexible. I raced down an aisle in the storage area, got to the end, and turned right. My mind raced. *No one has come in yet. Is there something I should be aware of? Are they waiting for me outside the door? Am I about to get zapped again? I've got to find a good place to hide!*

Just then I came into an area that appeared to be an MDI unit junkyard. I shuffled myself into a tight corner and hoped that 328 looked natural amongst the other units in various stages of disrepair. As I leaned against the wall gasping for breath, my heart pounded so loudly that I was sure the vibration could be felt throughout the building. Nothing happened.

I waited a long time until I was afraid I would miss Maria in the morgue. Still nothing happened.

I had a sudden stroke of genius, "What is your name?"
I whispered.

"There are no other beings in the room, so your
question is invalid," 328 replied.

I could have kissed that droid on the spot. Instead, I
began to cast about for something to make a frequency
converter. The first supply aisle I checked had scrubs of
every size and in five colors. I do not know what I had
expected them to look like, but the first thought that
popped into my mind was, *Two-hundred fifty years of
medical development and the scrubs look just like they
did in my day.* I grabbed a blue set in my size and began
the awkward dance to replace the open-backed gown
with the scrubs. Everything within me wanted to yank
that annoying probe out, but I knew that would trigger
an alert. And I figured I was working on borrowed time
as it was. *In a few minutes,* I assured myself, *then we'll
part ways.* I hoped I had not stated that out loud.

Next, I hurried into the first parts aisle and, sifting
through the shelves, it occurred to me that everything
was used. It had all come from other equipment. *This
place is a true junkyard*, I mused. *They must not be very
well funded.* Then I recalled they were a mission
hospital in what was described as the wasteland of
humanity. *Of course they're underfunded. They're
probably understaffed as well.*

That latter muse gave me a sense of relief, but did not
help me identify what I needed. Suddenly I remembered
that I was tethered to an information-searching
machine. "328, what components are in inventory here
at the hospital that could be used to make a frequency
converter from the local 20,000 hertz power to a 60
hertz power source?"

There seemed to be a lot of buzzing in 328's processor
before it responded. "Electronic components are not
inventoried in the hospital. The nearest source of such
equipment is the UC Power Authority warehouse,
Denver, Colorado."

I'm going to have to make this up as I go, I thought. *And I have to do it fast. How much time do I actually have?* I asked, "328, how long until the remains of Farren are slated for incineration?"

"Your question is too broad, there is no Farren in the data base who is scheduled for incineration. Please provide more detail," 328 replied.

I tried again, "328, What time is it and what is the schedule for remains' incineration in the morgue here?"

The response was chillingly casual, "The time is 6:45am. Incinerator schedule: Bronkowski, male, 9am. Johnston, male, 10am. Nelson, female, 11am. Unknown, unidentifiable remains, 12 noon. Vasquez, male, 1pm. Unknown, female, 2pm. Leighton, male, 3pm ... "

The machine kept listing the names, but I tuned it out. My mind was swimming in the reality that I had a mere five hours left to invent and build a charging device for my phone. For some unknown reason, I looked down at my scrubs and randomly had the thought to ask, "328, What are the color designations for hospital staff scrubs?"

The reply was, "The color designations of hospital scrubs are as follows: cleaning staff wears gray, nursing staff wears white, physicians wear yellow, maintenance staff wears green."

"What about the blue scrubs?" I asked, confused and a little bit concerned.

There was no reply. "328, who wears the blue scrubs?" I repeated with the correct format.

"Blue scrubs are worn by residents of the psychiatric unit," 328 responded, and I was almost certain I heard a hint of a snicker in that machine's voice.

"Oh my gosh! Maybe I really am nuts," I muttered as I raced back into the aisle looking for my size in green. My MDI unit tracked with me, but was in the next row over. I wondered if it was possible to slip out of the range of 328 with chess-style maneuvers. I fumbled through the scrubs in a panic.

My hand closed on the correct size and I yanked it out from under the pile and amazingly did not spill the rest onto the floor. I started to untie the shirt and a hand closed on my shoulder. "Gaaa!" I exclaimed as I launched to what should have been a three foot vertical flight. My feet never left the floor, but my heart went all the way to the roof. When I landed, my heart nearly stopped. A burly black man, in his mid-fifties, about six foot six, wearing green scrubs, had me by the shoulder. I knew resistance was pointless.

In a voice so gentle that I looked around to see if someone else was speaking, the man said, "Hey, buddy, what'cha doin' in here?"

I quickly looked the big man over and wondered that they made scrubs his size. "I think I got into the wrong scrubs. Are these blue? Or were those guys just messing with me because they know I'm colorblind?"

"Yep. They're blue," he replied. "Why do you want the green ones?"

"There's an urgent electrical problem to repair. And it's sort of right up my alley. Anyway, this is my first time out here and I guess Ms. Bergman wants all maintenance volunteers to wear the green scrubs." I tried to talk casually and hoped that my heartbeat was not audible to the man.

The big man chuckled and pointed to a tiny corner closet that I took to be a dressing locker. "You'd better change out of those blue ones or they'll think you're from the psychiatric unit."

A quick estimate reassured me the MDI unit would not need to move when I went to the changing room. I really did not need my droid shadow to expose my ruse to the big guy.

Inside the closet, I repeated my changing drill. *This guy could kill me with one punch,* I frantically thought. *I've got to keep him on the friendly side. Maybe he can help me get the parts I need.* I hastily formulated a plan and, as I exited the changing booth, I casually asked,

"So, are you tied up on a project or could I get you to give me a hand?"

"I can help," he replied. "I'm really good with electrical stuff."

Internally I clicked my heels with glee at that pronouncement. I nodded and asked, "Do you know your way around these parts bins pretty well?"

He nodded and watched with rapt attention as I sketched a rudimentary schematic on a notepad that was laying on a workbench. He continued to stare at the schematic as I jotted down a parts list. When I was almost done, he muttered, "You're making a transformer to step down the voltage to 120 volts AC with a freq-driver to step from 20,000 hertz to 60 hertz?"

My blood chilled a bit as I replied. "Yes. Then I need to invert to DC power and get a 2680 milliamp charge into a 3.8 volt battery to operate an old device."

"Hmm. For milliamp output on the DC side, it seems like it would be lots easier to just step across from a battery, like the ones they put in MDI units," the gentle giant replied. "They're 22.8 volts, weigh about 2.5 kilograms so they would be easy to transport. And they feed a 0.5 amp draw for nearly thirty hours."

It took a few seconds for his words to register. "A simple transformer buys me the time I need," I muttered under my breath.

He heard some of my mutterings, I knew not how much, and asked, "Is this time sensitive?"

"Desperately," I responded in a startlingly nonchalant tone. My mind was racing through the necessary steps and not emotionally engaged in the conversation. "Life and death desperate," I added.

"Coils are in the next aisle. Hand me that tester and we should be able to lay our hands on a six-to-one in a minute or two." His voice conveyed the urgency I had not expressed.

My curiosity about the man was piqued. "What do you do that brings you here as a volunteer?" I asked. "Where'd you get your electrical training?"

He regarded me with a look of suspicion for the first time and I wondered what I had said that was amiss. "I'm a patent attorney," he replied. "I specialize in electronics. And I have a client who is somewhat of a mad scientist. He invited me to help him develop a ... a secret project ... and he's the one who got me here." After a long pause he added, "So to speak."

I knew there was much more to the story and was suddenly curious. "That almost sounded like you are not pleased to be here. But what you are doing for these people is, is remarkable. You may never realize the impact you have on these inmates."

He looked wistfully at the tiny window and a protrusion just behind his ear was visible. I had a moment of terrifying realization. It was a chip, which meant the man was an inmate. He looked back with a resigned sigh and gave me a half smile. "Let's get your transformer made before it's too late."

We quickly assembled a crude transformer and borrowed an input plug from a retired MDI unit. I soldered two of the tiniest wires I could find to the output wires on the transformer, and sincerely hoped they would fit into the phone's charging port. "Ready," I stated.

"You're not colorblind," he replied calmly.

I gulped and tried to pretend I did not hear him. But the big man was looking at me like I owed him an explanation. Failing anything brilliant, I retorted, "You're not a volunteer."

He never blinked, but asked, "Why aren't you chipped?"

"What are you doing in this maintenance department?" I returned.

His expression never changed, and I was getting worried. He asked, "You're not from here, are you?"

I knew there was inferred meaning in his question, but did not want to overanswer, so I replied, "I don't belong here."

"Who are you?" he asked.

Waiting for a second to make sure I was not revealing too much, I stated, "Chadwick Thompson."

"What is your line of work?" he inquired.

"I'm an electronics developer … I've been called a mad scientist myself. Like your partner," I replied lamely.

"They think I'm insane, here," he whispered and began to sweat. I was suddenly afraid he was going to kill me on the spot. "They're coming for me," he gasped hoarsely. His face twisted into a grimace and, reaching up to the chip in his neck, the man began to tremble. Suddenly the door burst open.

I about freaked out as two security guards rushed in. One of them held one of the TASER-blaster weapons and the other held a scanning screen. I involuntarily flinched at the crack as the weapon was fired. The probe missed me by inches and stuck the big guy, taking him down like a giant sack of potatoes. The guards rushed past me and collected the big man.

"Are you okay, sir?" one of the guards asked me.

"Uh, yes, uh, yes, I'm, I'm fine," I stuttered. "Nice shot. It just missed me." My knees were shaking as I spoke.

"Wellsy here hasn't ever been violent, but you can't be too careful with a man this size. He wanders in here all the time," one of the guards explained as they sedated the man before removing the probe from his abdomen.

"Wellsy. Right. Well, I guess I never got his name. He was helping me with an improvised repair. He's actually a good electronics technician." I spoke in an avuncular manner as if I had allowed a child to help me. "If I need his help again, who do I ask for?"

"Haha! Thaddeus Willis, but everyone knows him as Wellsy." The guard gave me a knowing wink and mocked, "H.G. Wells here arrived in a time machine."

I must have looked dumbfounded, because the second guard explained, "It's from an old, old book."

I nodded and the first guard sarcastically added, "He's so crazy, he even makes his claims when he's sedated. I doubt he'd be of much use to you besides petty projects,

unless you want him to help you make a time machine."
Upon which both guards laughed hysterically.

"Bless his pea-pick'n heart," I added with a forced laugh.

The guards led the sluggish Wellsy away as he slurred, "Dr. Khatri is stuck in a time loop."

When the door to the shop closed I sank to the floor trembling. *This is beyond bizarre,* I thought. *I've got to get out of this place.* Then I suddenly remembered my charger project. Back at the bench, I plugged the makeshift transformer into an MDI battery and tested the output. *3.9 volts! Victory!*

I pulled out my phone to charge it and hit the status button. *100% charged,* it read. "100%! What? How can that be?" I exclaimed aloud. I checked Farren's phone, and it was at 100% also. "How can this possibly be?" I muttered in bewilderment. "328, how do batteries get charged in the hospital?" I asked.

328 replied, "Focal Impulse Charging light fixtures are employed throughout the hospital facility, affecting all recharging requirements up to 99.8 volts."

"You've got to be kidding me! I just spent half the day cobbing together a charger when my phone was already charged? Why did you not explain that to me earlier?" I snapped angrily.

There was a delay, then 328 responded, "Your question was too vague. Please clarify."

"328, do MDI units have a backup battery? Or do they go dormant when the battery is removed?" I asked almost too urgently.

"All MDI units are equipped with run-soft capacitors to operate emergency monitors for six minutes when the battery is removed for service," 328 reported. "No transmission or audio communication is available while in run-soft mode."

"Is the run-soft automatically engaged upon the removal of the battery, or is there a manual function necessary to save the data?" I asked.

My droid replied, "Switching to run-soft mode is automatic upon removal of the battery."

This is it, my friend 328. We're going to part ways now, I mused as I reached for the battery catch in my personal companion. But I thought of one more question before I unplugged the battery. "328, what room is Thaddeus Willis in?"

"Psychiatric patient Thaddeus Willis is registered in Room 199," the machine replied dutifully.

I reached for the battery catch again, but on an impulse I asked, "328, what happens with an MDI unit after six minutes without a battery?"

328 replied, "At six minutes, a distress locating beacon is transmitted and an alarm is activated to prevent the loss of data and monitoring capabilities. The welfare of the patient is the primary function of an MDI device."

I took a deep breath and looked around. *Six minutes,* I thought, *I'm going to have to really hustle.* I laid out the tools that I figured I would need to remove the probe. And I found one of the wound-healing hair dryers with a cracked housing. I wrapped it with duct tape and pressed the switch. It whirred like I thought it should sound. "It's go time," I said aloud as I pulled 328's battery from the unit. A series of lights blinked on that I took to be soft-run indicators.

I sliced the protective cuff off my arm, which turned out to be tougher than it appeared. Then I latched onto the probe with a pair of Vise-Grips and gave a gentle tug. I was amazed at how far the skin stretched. Grimly I thought, *This isn't going to be fun.* I yanked the probe, and all but cried out at the pain.

There was an alarming amount of blood and flesh attached to the probe barbs. I assumed there was a way to retract the barbs politely, but it was too late to figure that part out. I aimed the healing hair dryer at my arm and watched, once again, in utter amazement as the wound healed before my eyes.

"328, who invented the healing blow gun device?" I asked. But there was no reply, of course. I felt stupid. "Got to go, buddy." And I took off for the morgue.

The Morgue

I got to the morgue door exactly when the timer on my phone hit 3:00 minutes. "I've got three minutes before that thing rats me out," I mused under my breath as I reached for the doorknob.

The instant my fingers made contact with the knob, the lights dimmed, a red beacon began flashing, and a shriek alarm went off. A message was broadcast across the intercom, but I was too panicked to understand what was being said. I heard my own voice shouting furiously, "I was supposed to have three more minutes! What's going on?"

I was suddenly shaken to the floor by a sharp tremor, and I thought someone had crashed into me with the morgue door. But the door was still closed. I was bewildered. Another tremor shook the place a few seconds after the first. The concussion was so hard a crack developed in the floor under my face. "Oh, no! That's not good!" I exclaimed to no one. I abruptly realized that the hospital was under siege. *Someone is firing mortars at a hospital?* My brain pirouetted around the paradox.

I regained my feet and tried the door, but it was jammed from the buckling in the floors and walls. Someone body slammed me, sort of, and I found myself being rushed down the hallway between two anxious-looking security guards. "This way, sir! This way! To the trains! We've got to evacuate now!" one of them was shouting into my ear over the chaos.

Somehow I finally heard the message on the intercom repeating, "All volunteers and personnel report to the train for immediate evacuation! Last train launch in 2 minutes 12 seconds! All volunteers and personnel report to the train for immediate evacuation! Last train launch in 2 minutes 10 seconds! All volunteers and personnel report to the train for immediate evacuation! Last train launch in 2 minutes 8 seconds!"

There were several more tremors and the hallways began to fill with fine dust. The combination of flashing red lights in the airborne dust made an eerie, even surreal, scene as we pressed down the last hallway. Inmates were being tazed to prevent them from getting past the security gates, and I saw my big friend Thaddeus take a double charge to stop him. The chaos was incomprehensible. My guards whisked us through the security gates, and we were abruptly enveloped by the panicked crowd in an underground train bay. My mind raced to assemble logic out of what I was seeing. *It's a subway. That makes sense if they need to get into and out of this prison without letting the inmates out.*

Somehow I was squeezed onto the last subway car only about ten passengers before the last person was on and the door was closed. I looked out the window in time to see several guards, who had stayed behind to hold the doorway, furiously firing TASER darts into inmate after inmate. I saw Thaddeus take another hit from the TASER and almost cried out for him. "That man is unbelievably tough," I whispered.

As the train began to move, the guards were overrun, and I had the crushing realization that they had sacrificed their lives to save the rest of the volunteers. And somehow I had been mistaken for one of them.

Everyone in the car gasped at the sudden ferocity of the assault. And one woman, who was leaning against the window, openly sobbed at the sight of the guards being beaten to death. Then the train launched into the tunnel. The click of the wheels and the woman sobbing were the only sounds that could be heard. I was in complete shock.

It did not last long. There was another tremor, only it was much more palpable. And the subway came to a screeching halt, coming within inches of striking the car ahead. A glance revealed that a long line of cars was stopped. Relief flooded me as I first assumed we were at the station, but that feeling melted quickly. There was a general stir in the car, then a second wave of panic set in. About eight cars ahead, light was coming in from a crater over the car. It could only be coming from the surface and, by the amount of motion, it appeared that soldiers were coming into the tube.

An intercom crackled and a panicked voice called out, "Security! The tube has been breached! Armed New England gangs are descending into the train tube! Is there any security available?" The crack of automatic gunfire could be heard in the background, and I could not tell if it was coming over the radio or if we were hearing it echo in the tube. A spray of bullets smashed into the windshield of our subway car, answering that question.

As I irrationally marveled that the windshield could deflect the bullets, a radio response came back. "Security is on the way!" And a follow-up of TASER ray-gun crackles accompanied the transmission. We could only see the skirmish obliquely around the other cars, but I was alarmed that it appeared there were hundreds of surface gang members streaming into the tube. I knew there was no way the non-lethal TASERs could hold off the numbers of assailants attacking the cars.

It seemed to happen all at once that the radios erupted in panicked calls for help. The security volunteers were inevitably overwhelmed by the sheer number of combatants and the ferocity of the assault. We could see them going from car to car shooting the doors until the hasps failed. When each one opened, several members would rush in and the chaos was terrifying.

I pulled out my phone and began to key in a jump, when a hand touched my shoulder. "Is this your handiwork, Mr. Thompson? Is this the work of your weapon? Are you satisfied with your flippant responses now?" Ms. Bergman's accusing voice took me up short. I realized then that she was the one who had been weeping at the window.

"It's Dr. Thompson," I snapped, unintentionally venting my stress. "And this is not a weapon! Your conflict here has nothing to do with me or my phone! This is the depth of depravity! Surely you, as a missionary in the darkest place on earth, understand that concept."

But in that instant, I realized that my phone had everything to do with the conflict. It all came to me in a rush. *Those guys had seen something spectacular. They saw Farren appear as if he had materialized from thin air, then he vanished before their eyes. The phone was left amid his remains and the mission got it. Then a few hours later, the same "magic trick" was repeated. Only we did not vanish. They want my phone.*

"They want my phone," I said half under my breath. Then, looking at the beleaguered woman, I urged, "They're coming for me and my phone. They are going to kill every one of us to get it. If you want me to save your life, touch my arm."

Tears streamed down her face as she gestured toward the crowded subway. Her choked reply was, "I want someone to save their lives, Mr. Thompson!"

The gunfire was getting much closer, and I found myself flinching at the sounds. Impatiently I snapped back, "I can't save their lives, Ms. Bergman. I can only save yours. Then you can save theirs!"

"That is no longer possible, sir," she wept.

"Touch me now! I'm jumping back in time twenty minutes! You can evacuate the premises before the assault begins!" I reasoned desperately. It seemed logical in my mind.

She looked aghast and, beyond any rational imagination, she argued with me. "You would deign to tread into God's sovereign realms of life and death and time and, and … that's not our place, Mr. Thompson! It's, it's … blasphemous!"

"Listen, lady," I snapped way too rudely, "No one has or ever will wrestle the sovereignty out of God's hands! What's wrong with you? Don't you go to Sunday School? That's inherent in the definition of God!" Ear-splitting machine-gun fire ripped through the door latch of our car, and several people fell screaming from bullet and shrapnel wounds. "If you don't touch my arm this instant, you will seal the death of every one of your people!" I screamed over the numbing sounds, then I pressed the button.

Room 199

I had not consciously realized that I had been kneeling when I pressed the jump button, until I landed half on a chair, knees first. I hit the floor with a crash and jumped up to see Thaddeus Willis, wide-eyed, in his bed. He looked to be about half drunk, and I knew the sedative he had been given was still affecting him.

"Oh! Oh! Dear God, forgive us!" Ms. Bergman cried. "What have we done?"

I hastily helped her up. And without any further explanation, I jerked my thumb toward the door. "Sound the evacuation alarm. We're in Room 199. You have seventeen and a half minutes before the first mortar hits," I ordered.

She started to faint and I caught her before she went down. "Evacuate now! We've got to get going," I urged Bergman.

I glanced at my phone. The charge said 100%. *I'm loving this light beam impulse whatever-it-is technology,* I thought. Then I pulled the big man to the edge of his bed and realized he was in blue scrubs. *No time to change that now,* I thought. "Thaddeus, come on. Quickly, let's go, and tell me about your time travel, um, experience, or theory. Let's go."

I looked over at Bergman who was leaning against a chair and hyperventilating. I said, "Mortars ... bombs are coming. You've got just under 17 minutes before the first one hits! Evacuate now!"

Somehow she regained her composure enough to address something in the room, "Initiate Code Red Evacuation." And like a scenario of dèjá vu, everything busted loose. Lights, alarms, and panicked people started over and I wished I had made it to the morgue before it all happened.

I did not have time to wait around, so I took off, leading my friend as fast as he could go. "I've seen you before," he said.

"Yes, we worked together on a transformer in the maintenance shop," I replied.

He shook his head. "No, I've seen your picture. You're Dr. Chadwick Thompson. The famous inventor and developer of the twenty-first century. I researched your time machine."

I stopped in the chaotic flood of people who were rushing the opposite direction we were going. "How? Where did you ever find that?" I blurted.

"Dr. Khatri found your notes and drawings in the bottom of a safe he bought at an antique shop. That was in '50, 2250. He conscripted me to help decipher and ultimately to build a time travel machine. We did a test run in 2255. I'm thirty-three years old and look at me, I look like I'm fifty-five. I did all the research back in the archives, but there wasn't a lot of info on the time machine. We had to make a couple of broad assumptions, but it worked on the first launch. When we landed, in this time, some wires were damaged. We had made everything external for safety's sake. When I got the wires fixed, I accidentally launched, or more likely vaporized, the box with Dr. Khatri in it. I think I cross-shorted the time polarizer wires. I'm not sure, it happened so fast. But now I'm afraid the doctor is lost in a time loop."

I stopped again at the morgue door. And, trying to clear my head, I said, "This is all kind of freaking me out. Let me get this all straight. I'm basically 200 years, plus or minus, past my lifetime, and here you are from a whole different time, talking about a machine that was made from my notes ... a couple hundred years ago, which I maybe haven't written yet! And you recognized me, because you've seen my picture somewhere in your research."

Thaddeus nodded. I looked over at Ms. Bergman and she shrugged with a hopelessly bewildered look. Suddenly I realized Bergman was following us. "Ms. Bergman! You've got to evacuate! Go! Run!"

"I'm not leaving without you," she stated stubbornly.

"We can't go on the train. We're inmates," I pleaded.

"You can come with me," she insisted.

"Look, we're leaving by a time travel machine. You've got about eleven minutes before the first mortar. And I've lost track of the train time," I retorted. "You have to go."

"I'm staying beside you until you are safely gone. It's my duty to assure the safety of everyone in the hospital," she stated doggedly.

"You know these halls are going to be flowing with blood in about twenty minutes, right?" I asked bluntly.

She wiped away the tears from her eyes as she nodded, and I had the distinct sense that she was going to go down with her ship, if it came to that. I turned to the task ahead and pushed the door open. It was much quieter in the morgue. *No evacuation alarm in here? I mused. I guess they must not have expected to have a lot of evacuees from the room full of dead people.*

Maria startled from dutifully doing her chores in the morgue when we walked in. She looked furtively from me to Ms. Bergman, but there was no reprimand. "Why haven't you evacuated?" I blurted.

The woman looked up at me and explained, "Señor, I am an inmate. There is no place for me to go."

I was astonished at how graciously she accepted her fate without a hint of despair.

"Help me find Farren and Tanya please," I asked without addressing anyone.

Bergman went directly to a drawer and slid it open. There were only bones in a wire mesh bag. "This was the first of the unidentified remains. The device was with this one," she stated. Then pulling another drawer,

she pointed at Tanya's remains and gave me a
questioning glance.

"Tanya," I gasped and tried unsuccessfully to hold back
the tears. She was also confined inside a wire mesh that
I took to be used in the incinerator. "I need to get them
close enough to touch them both." Even as I said it, I
realized they were locked into the drawers.

I looked to Bergman. She shook her head. "I don't have
those keys. And he's probably on the train by now."

I pointed at her and demanded, "You, get to the train
now! That's an order!"

She glanced at a timepiece and casually replied, "I've
got six more minutes before the last train. I need three
to get there. What else do you need?"

My mind was swirling, and the remembrance of the
imminent mortar attack did not help me think clearly. "I
don't know. I don't know. Are there tools nearby that we
can use to cut the wire mesh?" I asked.

Bergman shook her head, then asked, "If someone is
touching you and also touching the other remains, is
that a sufficient contact for your machine?"

All eyes turned to me. "I think so," I hesitated, then, on
the edge of panic, I continued my horrible thought. "But
that can't work. I'm the only one here with Dr. Nelson's
serum to prevent linear aging." I looked from Bergman,
to Thaddeus, to Maria. "I've got to choose between
Farren and Tanya," I choked out in dismay.

Unimaginable Sacrifice

Bergman rushed from the room and I realized her time was up. I was not sure what to do with Thaddeus or Maria at that moment. I was slowly comprehending that my escapade was going to cost someone his or her life. And it was likely to be several someones. I shut the thought from my mind so I could think clearly.

In a flurry of thoughts, I debated, *If I take Farren, and can somehow resuscitate him, there is some chance he and I can figure out a way to undo all that has happened. If not, I've chosen the path of most destruction.*

Looking at his pile of dry bones did not give me much hope. *If I take Tanya, I have to decide between leaving her in her proper time zone where she will forget me when I undo the event in her time. Or, breaking all of what seems morally right, we could start over in my time zone and she would have a full, day-by-day memory of the next thirty-odd years. And somehow I have left Thaddeus to die a violent death in a foreign time zone because he found some of my documents. But, there is some possibility that I could destroy all of my notes and undo his demise. No, since he's dead in one time zone, he's dead in all of them.*

I looked up from my desperate musing to see Maria praying and Thaddeus watching me. "We're going to die, aren't we?" he asked. He seemed surprisingly calm.

I took a deep breath to make my voice not shake, but, before I could reply, Bergman bustled back in. "My gosh, woman! You are stubborn! Run! Save yourself!" I practically yelled at her.

"Too late," she casually stated, then, snapping up
Thaddeus's sleeve, she injected him with a syringe.

I had never seen a black man turn so pale, but he
somehow did not fall over. That was a good thing,
because none of us could have caught him. "There you
go, big guy. Cancer free for the next decade." Then
turning to Maria, she ordered, "You're next."

Maria fearlessly took the shot, then Bergman directed,
"Do your thing, time jumper. Get these people out of my
hospital." Then she stepped back with a look that
conveyed she was prepared to accept her own,
undoubtedly brutal, death.

Maria touched Tanya's body, Thaddeus touched
Farren's bones, and they each touched me. With the
three of us, it was just the right amount of reach.
Bergman had thought it through brilliantly. *That's why
she's the director,* I thought. Suddenly I had an idea.
"Bergman, if you could inject yourself, I can take you
out, then bring you back fifteen minutes ago. I can drop
you near the trains and jump back out."

She looked at me quizzically. "I was ready to have you
burned for witchcraft a few hours ago," she replied in
amazement. "Now you're trying to save my life?"

"What? They do that now?" I asked incredulously.

She grabbed both of my arms and exclaimed,
"Figuratively! Now go!"

"You can't make up for that with your own blood. You
know better than that," I argued.

I could tell a question was forming, but just then the
first mortar hit. She turned and sprinted out of the
room. The door had spring hinges, so it began to close.
And on an impulse, I ran and pulled the door open just
in time for the second mortar to crack the floor. The
door jammed open. In seconds, Bergman came rushing
back in and handed me the syringe. "I can't do me," she
stated.

I stalled, but Thaddeus snatched the syringe and, like a
pro, injected Bergman. She swayed slightly, but I
steadied her before she fell. Everyone assumed their

respective positions and I had one more idea. "Can we try to heal Tanya's wounds with one of those hair-dryer-looking things that makes wounds heal in seconds?"

Bergman looked confused, "A SCFM? Stem Cell Frequency Multiplier? Cell cloning device?"

"Yeah," I nodded.

"That only works on living cells. It won't have any effect on her," Bergman explained as another mortar shook the building.

"It's the best chance I've got to resuscitate her," I urged desperately. "She has the anti-aging serum in her system, and I was thinking her cells might still be responsive."

Shaking her head doubtfully, Bergman stepped out of the morgue again and returned with a triage cart. She grabbed a cell cloning device and "shot" it at Tanya's fatal wounds. "Oh, my gosh!" she exclaimed. "Stem cells treated with FN serum apparently do not telegraph the death code immediately." She looked at us and explained, "When a person dies, there is a cell ripple, a chain reaction signal, if you will, that switches the cells into death mode. It's like turning off a long water hose. But, this ... this is amazing." Another mortar interrupted the lesson. "Quickly! Transfusion!" And Bergman grabbed a box with a couple of hoses protruding from each end.

"I don't know her blood type," I called out urgently over the noises that were increasing down the hallway.

She stabbed my arm and muttered, "How could such medically illiterate barbarians from the Dark Ages invent time travel?"

The box whirred and I felt my blood pumping into the machine. I could see it going into Tanya's arm. "Automatically filters and corrects for blood type?" I asked.

She made a face and replied, "Sort of. It's a bit more involved than that. Each blood cell is stripped to its fundamental code and reassembled to match the encoding of the recipient."

I nodded dumbly. The whole thing took less that a minute. "Okay, heart impulse time," Bergman ordered.

I stood up to help, but was a little dizzy from the blood loss. Bergman was like a cyclone zipping around. She handed me a bottle and ordered, "Drink."

As I guzzled the contents, she applied the defibrillator-looking device. In what seemed like a dream, I watched as Tanya's body arched from the electric impulse. Nothing happened. Bergman repeated the procedure with the same results. The noises down the hallway were almost to the morgue, and Bergman ordered, "Let's jump now."

I turned and saw Maria hastily get up from her knees. *That woman was praying this whole time*, I thought. *Bless her.* Someone shouted through the doorway as I pressed the button. The sound of gunfire was cut off abruptly. My last thought was, *I hope this many people jumping doesn't crash the battery.*

The Second Dark Age

The battery did not crash. We all landed in Dr. Nelson's office in a jumble, and Dr. Nelson stated, "Sixty seconds. You missed the prime by one second." He sounded genuinely disappointed.

I jumped up and nearly shouted, "Dr. Nelson! We've got a bit of an emergency here!"

Bergman leaned against a wall and gasped, "When am I at?"

"2048," I responded. "We need to get an AED on Tanya now!" I demanded.

Maria found a corner and began her prayer vigil again. I was secretly comforted by that. Thaddeus looked lost, but intrigued. "This is like a museum," he said with a voice full of wonder.

I realized no one was in any condition to help me much, so I grabbed the wire mesh bag with Farren's remains and dragged them carefully to one side. I touched Tanya's face and realized the wire bag had not come with. *Odd*, I mused, *I wonder if Thaddeus's big hand contacted enough square inches of the wire mesh for the signal to be an electronically significant contact.*

"I'm so sorry," I whispered again. "I'm trying to bring you back." I began chest compressions on her as I heard Dr. Nelson call on the intercom for an AED.

In seconds, Eyelash Marsha was there with the device. She immediately went into shock at the scene, but I did not have time to think about her feelings at that point. Ms. Bergman had recovered from her initial shock, and took over the administration of the defibrillator. She repeated the performance that had been begun in her morgue. I told Dr. Nelson the abbreviated version of our experience, and he dispassionately took it all in. After several shocks, Ms. Bergman pronounced that it was not working.

Dr. Nelson was standing by, watching as if he intended to make an unbiased report of the incident. When Bergman made her heart-wrenching pronouncement, Dr. Nelson sat down and casually processed the data aloud. "We know that her DNA had not signaled it was dead. But in physical reality it was dead. So the electrical impulses are being fired into cells that somehow know they are in a dead body. There has been some transmission of that information, so perhaps it is the nerve signals that are confused. I'm formulating a theory that the reintroduction of her native DNA, that was taken and suspended in its living state, will jump-start the resuscitation of the cells."

He then casually removed a sample from his specimen freezer and loaded a syringe with a long thin needle. I was captivated, even though I was sure my heart had stopped. He knelt beside Tanya and said, "Dr. Blake, my dear old friend, I think we're about to see you come back to life." He then inserted the needle into her heart and I almost threw up. Standing to his feet, he instructed Ms. Bergman, "You may proceed now."

It was so different that time, I broke down into tears. The recoil from the AED shock landed Tanya sideways, gasping for breath. Everything got crazy for a few minutes, and I felt Ms. Bergman pulling on my arms, which were wrapped around Tanya. I did not remember moving to her.

"You've got to let her breathe, Mr. Thompson! You're crushing the breath back out of her!" Ms. Bregman was crying as she wrested my arms loose.

Maria was all smiles and declared that she was the luckiest person alive to see two miracles in one day.

When everything stabilized, Tanya, in a weak voice, asked me, "Did we find Farren?"

I cried some more and told her we had. I did not have the heart to tell her it was way too late for him. I helped her into a soft-looking loveseat and grabbed a lab coat from a hook to cover her tattered clothes.

"I guess I need another change of clothes," she said wryly. "Unless bullet-riddled and blood-soaked is suddenly back in fashion."

Nothing about her statement was actually humorous, but I laughed out loud at the word picture it conjured in my head. I think the comic relief did some good to clarify my mind, because immediately after that I looked around the room. *Where to begin?* I thought. *The charger.* I tossed my phone into the charger and looked at Bergman. "You first?" I asked.

She nodded. "But first I need to remove the chips from them," she gestured toward Maria and Thaddeus.

A scalpel and sutures were produced by Dr. Nelson. Bergman looked at the needle and thread with disdain. It may as well have been a jar of leeches and a set of bloodletting lancets by the look on her face. I had a wild idea and got my phone. "I'll be back in … seven seconds." Dr. Nelson smiled ever so slightly.

I landed four minutes before we left and grabbed the SCFM from the floor where it had fallen. When I returned, I had expected the cutting to be finished. But Bergman had been stunned by my abrupt disappearance, and even more shaken when I suddenly reappeared in the seventh second. I handed her the device, and she quickly cut the chips from Maria and Thaddeus, healing the cuts with her magic hair dryer.

Meanwhile, I had recharged my phone for the jump out again, and when she had gathered the various vestiges of her time, Ms. Bergman bid her farewells. Maria hugged her, and I knew that did the administrator's troubled heart some good. We jumped to Room 199. We were welcomed by the shrieking alarms and strobing lights, and I could hear the countdown to the last trains' scheduled departure.

I shook Ms. Bergman's hand and warned her, "I'm sorry that you have to bear the burden of this secret. If you **ever** tell anyone what happened, they will lock you up in here," I waived in the direction of the psychiatric ward. "And they will forget about you." I nodded as I yelled toward her. When she nodded affirmation, I added, "I'm sorry I can't set your time back to what it was. Without Farren," I choked on that thought, "we can't jump in prior to his arrival and jump back out without stirring up interest. And the truth is, I don't even know if that would actually work."

Again I nodded to get her feedback. She nodded in return. I wished I could make up for my destruction somehow, but the sense of overwhelming disaster was all around us and quite impossible to ignore. All I could say in parting was, "I'm so sorry for this. Your work here has been truly amazing."

"God be with you, Dr. Thompson," she said with all the graciousness I imagined Mother Theresa would have conveyed.

I nodded and replied, "And with you also." I looked at my phone and it was already at 100% charge. I pointed at the door expectantly. But she just gave me a defiant look and pointed at my phone. I smiled at the obstinate woman and realized I had developed a tremendous respect for her in a short amount of time. I pushed the return button.

Tijuana

Back in Dr. Nelson's office, I tossed my phone into the charger again, and decided for the next jumps I would start and land beside the charger. It was a trivial thought, but such things come to mind when one is in the midst of great stress.

"Maria, where in Tijuana do you want to go?" I asked when I had my phone ready.

"You can't go to Tijuana," Dr. Nelson reminded me. "The power supply and recharging capabilities may be inadequate. You might not be able to get back."

Triumphantly I replied, "For once, I'm ahead of you on something." I held up the battery out of Farren's phone. "One battery out and one back."

Dr. Nelson gave me an approving nod. "Excellent," he replied. "It is fully charged?"

I double checked and it was. Maria showed me on the map where her family home was, and I keyed in the coordinates. She hugged Tanya like a long-lost sister, and tearfully took my arm. Through tears, Tanya said, "Don't be hugging on him too much now."

We were laughing when I hit the button. Tijuana in 2276 was a scary-looking place. I hastily changed batteries and asked, "Are you sure you want to be left here?"

She nodded, and a large, militant-looking man emerged from a doorway. He was holding what I took to be a weapon. "Maria! ¿Quién es ese hombre?" he asked.

"Un amigo," she replied.

The man looked at me and nodded. I nodded in return. "Are you okay here?" I asked.

"Yes, my brother will take care of me now," she responded with a smile. She gave me a hug, and then a second hug. "That one is to give to your wife from me," she said as she stepped back and waved.

I nodded and pressed the return button. I did not have the time to correct Maria's assumption about my relationship status with Tanya.

When I had tossed my phone and the spare battery into the charger, I turned my attention to Thaddeus. The instant I was about to speak, I remembered an omission from my questions for Ms. Bergman. "Aw, man! I forgot to ask how that cell cloning thingy worked. That is one thing that could be a real lifesaver. I mean, it was a lifesaver. Back there, in the future." I cut my losses and shut up.

Thaddeus looked at me like I had just dropped in from Mars. "Man, that's really old technology. Your son invented it. When I ran across that article in my research, I thought it was really interesting that you and your son both had so many inventions that shook the world. I got a particular kick out of the fact that we had the same name too."

"We have the same name?" I asked, confused.

"Your son and I. You just don't meet a lot of Thaddeuses, you know," the big man replied with a grin.

I could not speak. *The medical device that saved my life before I have a son, had been invented by my son.* My mind was profoundly boggled. *Will I have a son? I have to meet someone who will marry me first. Do I even know any unmarried women? I'm kind of running out of time, biologically speaking. What happens if I don't ever have a son?* I just smiled and nodded until I could regain control of my voice.

Just then a young woman gingerly opened the door about halfway. "Dr. Nelson?" she hesitantly interrupted. He stood up and I realized he was nervous. "I brought you a chai tea … it's breaktime …"

The girl from the mail room, I thought. Glancing at Tanya, I knew my assumption was correct. For some reason, I could not look away from Tanya. Her face seemed to glow, and I realized in that instant that she was indeed wired to be a relational counselor. Sadly, she had wasted her life as a prison examiner. *No wonder she was so bitter,* I thought.

Weakly, Tanya said, "I'm thirsty too." And I realized I had not eaten anything in about forty-eight hours.

I jumped up and said, "I'll get you something. Coffee? Orange juice?"

"No," Dr. Nelson insisted. "For the purposes of damage control, you all need to stay in this room. Miss Carson and I will bring you all food and beverages." And with that, they whisked out of the room.

His desk phone rang almost immediately. *That is so predictably ironic,* I mused in exasperation. The three of us stared at it like dogs waiting for something to drop from the kitchen counter. Mercifully it stopped, as such things tend to do, and Tanya slid to one side of the little couch.

If Maria had been there, she would have witnessed a third miracle that day, because I actually took a hint. Sitting down beside Tanya, she snuggled up to me, and I felt like my face was turning red. "You need a change of clothes too," she whispered. I nodded.

Thaddeus asked, "How long have you kids been married?"

My jaw went slack and I thought, *That is hysterical coming from someone who is my junior by a couple of centuries.*

"We met in a prison psych ward," she replied, toying with the big man's sense of humor. I was a few seconds behind the curve before I realized that she was actually toying with me.

He smirked and remarked, "We did too. Sort of." He laughed, then added, "But that was back before you were alive. Does he do that often?"

Just then the door opened, and Dr. Nelson and Miss Carson walked in with sandwiches from the deli, along with coffees and a hot chocolate. I had never been so hungry in my life. We ate in silence and it was like Thanksgiving dinner to me.

Naturally, Tanya was the one who thought to make all the introductions. Interestingly, she began with Melissa Carson, then she went to Thaddeus. I waited an awkward amount of time to be introduced before I stated, "And I'm Chadwick Thompson."

"Oh. I've heard all about you, Dr. Thompson," Melissa replied with a girlish giggle.

I glanced sidelong at Tanya and she gave me an *"I'm so innocent"* look. And punctuated it with a wink. I regained my wits and said, "It's just Chad. If you don't mind. Among friends." And I gestured around the group with a glance.

We all sat with that awkward silence that so often happens when a private conversation has been interrupted. Finally Melissa stood and, with eyes darting back and forth between Tanya and me, said, "Well, it's been very nice to meet you all. I've got to get back to work."

Once again it was Tanya who rescued the moment. "Oh, I'll replace the outfit. Sorry, it's sort of messed up. Would you rather have a direct replacement, or a shopping card?"

"Oh! No! I wasn't worried about that," she hastily replied. "Henrik ... um, Dr. Nelson said he would take care of that. I was just wondering if you all are part of a historical reenactment. The makeup and blood stains look really real."

I looked at Tanya for help and, without missing a beat, she answered, "It is something like that, but very futuristic."

Melissa seemed to light up and almost squealed, "Oh! Time travel cosplay! That is so cool! We should do that, Henrik!"

Dr. Henrik Nelson was in way over his head with that one. I was equal parts amused and mortified by the sudden imbalance in the room. I laughed nervously and Thaddeus looked aghast. Again Tanya rolled right along with it. "It has its moments," she acknowledged, "but currently it's a closed group until the ground rules are established."

As Melissa prattled on about how much fun we must be having, I just thought about Tanya. *How does she do that? It's like she always knows the right thing to say.*

After an eternity or so, Melissa went back to work. She was actually quite likable and there was certainly nothing wrong with the girl. But, after that high-emotion, low-intellectual display of character, I suspected Dr. Nelson might be falling out of love with her. I was wrong.

"What a refreshing light she sheds on things," Dr. Nelson remarked to no one in particular. Then to Tanya he asked, "Is it too soon to ask her for a date? Is the Inventors' Congress a good place to start?"

With a slight chuckle Tanya replied, "No and no. Dinner and theater. Either drama or humor."

He nodded. "I see," was all he replied. Then, turning his attention to Thaddeus, Dr. Nelson said, "Now, tell us about your time machine and what went amiss."

Busted

Thaddeus began with how Dr. Khatri had come upon my notes and drawings when he purchased an antique safe at an auction. He had become intrigued with the notion of time jumping and had conscripted Thaddeus to assist in the electrical development of the time morphing mechanism. When they had completed the machine, Dr. Khatri selected a date twenty-one years into the future and a location not far from the border of the New England Penitentiary. They made the jump successfully, but upon landing, the machine sustained some external damage to the wiring. While Thaddeus had worked to repair the wires, Dr. Khatri had reset the destination for home. At that point, there was some unintentional short and the box, with Dr. Khatri in it, had disappeared from before Thaddeus's eyes.

When Thaddeus finished his account of the event, Dr. Nelson summarized the details. "So, in 2249, Dr. Khatri, a prosthetic inventor, found some cryptic two-hundred-year-old notes and determined to build a time travel machine from them?"

Amending the fact, Thaddeus interrupted, "I should admit that he brought the drawings for me to research. That's where I found out so much about Dr. Thompson and his prodigious portfolio of inventions. It was my idea to try to replicate the time morphing mechanism."

"You're an attorney?" Dr. Nelson asked to clear some illogical bit from his assemblage of data.

"I am a patent attorney specializing in electronic inventions. I also have a degree in electrical engineering," the big man clarified.

"Okay, that makes more sense now. So, you jumped from 2255 to 2276. What was the significance of that date and location?" Dr. Nelson sounded like a lawyer going for the throat at the moment.

"That was Dr. Khatri's decision. I was just along as tech support. Well, I was curious about the ride too," Thaddeus responded.

"Describe your power supply and draw," Dr. Nelson said, more like an order than request.

Technical questions were right up Thaddeus's alley. He perked up and explained, "We were powered by a 4G regenerative carbon cell generator. Those generators came along well after your time. Our consumption making the jump out cost us about 63% of capacity. So we technically needed twenty-four hours to fully regen. But we actually could have made up enough power to make the reverse jump, counting what was in the reserve, in eight hours. That would have landed us totally flat, but back home in time and space. As it was, we were on the ground, so to speak, for only about three hours."

Dr. Nelson had one more question. "Are you certain that the return destination was identical to your origin?"

"Yes. I had to manually enter all of the coding into the chips and there were only two options. It was a laborious task. I am in awe of what Dr. Thompson has done here in the Dark Ages. His little machine is a wonder."

"Why do people keep calling our time the Dark Ages?" I asked somewhat annoyed. "That was like six hundred years ago."

"Buddy," the big man said with a smile, "History has branded your era the Second Dark Age. I'm just repeating what has been taught in schools for decades."

Tanya remarked, "They're probably not too far off the mark."

I had the impulse to remind her of how civilized the world was when she died in my arms, but realizing we had been in the anarchical prison grounds of the world,

I thought better of it. Instead, I asked, "Where can we get some different clothing?"

Dr. Nelson seemed to come out of his reverie for a moment and said, "Of course. I'll call Marsha and have her get Melissa to help you."

There was a light knock on the door and, when Dr. Nelson called out, Melissa entered looking rather pale. "Henrik? Your phone was on, and I kept trying to get your attention, and … Are you in some kind of trouble?"

"On?" Dr. Nelson asked, confused.

"I think you must have hit the stick-call button when I gave you my number," she replied self-consciously. "I wasn't trying to get in the middle of someone else's business."

Tanya gave me a surprised look. "This is a giant step for him," she whispered. I nodded, even though my mind was spinning through our conversation which had been overheard. *This can't be good*, I thought.

Dr. Nelson was looking at his phone like a novice. It was obvious he did not get out much. "Can you help them get some fresh clothes?" he asked. It was clear that he did not recognize Melissa's distress.

Wide-eyed, Melissa nodded, then asked, "Are you all actually time travelers, for real, and not cosplayers?"

I felt like a possum in the headlights. Looking up from his phone, Dr. Nelson replied casually, "It's true, and I can explain it all."

"Then that's actually, real … blood? Are you going to be okay?" she asked, pointing at Tanya.

Tanya nodded, and I thought she was going to be stumped for the first time. But she gently responded, "I was killed a couple of hundred years from now. They brought me back here and resuscitated me. I'm fine now. Thank you, sweetie, for being concerned."

There was a moment of magic in Tanya's words and Melissa seemed to recover remarkably well.

"That is so cool," Melissa whispered breathlessly. Then clouding up a bit, she said, "I heard Marsha on the phone with the police. They're probably on their way here now. Do you think this will be a problem?"

I bounded to my feet so fast Melissa started with a gasp.

"Time to jump!" I ordered. "We've got to figure out how to retrieve Dr. Khatri from the time loop. Dr. Nelson, when can we return? Is twenty minutes ago sufficient?" I reached for Tanya's hand as Thaddeus hurried to my side.

As I keyed in the time for our return, Melissa said, "Henrik, if you will select 'Unstick Call,' I can use my phone to call Daddy. He's a lieutenant in the police department. He may be able to call them off."

I heard sirens in the distance and thought, *Why do people romanticize time travel so much? I've been tazed so many times, in so many different time zones, I could get a job as the Energizer Bunny.*

Melissa showed Dr. Nelson how to unstick the call from his phone, and in seconds she was talking to her father. I overheard, "Yes, Daddy, I'm fine. Well, we have a lady here who is maybe a little high-strung. She seems to think someone from outer space, or some time traveler, is invading the place. Yes, he's fine. We actually had lunch together today. He's really nice. Yes. Of course."

Meanwhile, the sirens had stopped at our building, and I could hear a commotion below. I hovered my finger over the button, but for some reason did not jump. I strained to ascertain more from Melissa's side of the conversation. "Yes, he's right here. Actually, I'm in his office with several of his colleagues. They are all such geniuses. It's sort of a nerd-fest, but I'm really enjoying it. Oh, you're on the call. Of course. Come on up, I'll be happy to introduce you. He'll be pleased to meet you too. Level 3, Room 19. Love you too. See you in a minute."

Melissa dropped her pen-phone into her pocket and looked at Dr. Nelson, beaming. "You're going to get to meet my dad. He's on his way up."

The sirens all stopped, but Dr. Nelson looked like he had seen a ghost. I glanced right and left. They both had good contact with me. "Touch them," I ordered. Tanya touched Melissa and Thaddeus reached his big arm across the desk and touched Dr. Nelson. I pressed the button.

Another Brush with the Law

That was the first time I had done a jump from and to the exact same location. It was almost more confusing because, other than a brief whiteout, nothing changed, except the clock. Melissa looked stunned.

"Okay, people. We have twenty minutes and roughly seventeen seconds before an armed lawman walks through that door. We need to get Tanya some clothes that are not blood-soaked. And we need to look like we belong here. And … we need to remove Farren's remains." I sounded like a sergeant barking orders before a mission.

Melissa looked at Tanya with an apologetic expression and asked, "Will you be okay with a gym outfit? It's fresh out of the laundry." Tanya nodded, but it was not like there was time for any other options. Melissa took off for her locker, and it occurred to me that we were all completely dependent on the performance of the only non-scientist in the group.

I pointed to Dr. Nelson and ordered Tanya, "Coach him." She immediately began conversational role-playing with the stratospheric genius. I was amused to think, *Oddly enough, the smartest person in the room, maybe on the planet, is completely incapable of making small talk.*

Thaddeus and I cleared off a table and laid Farren's remains, still in the wire mesh bag, on the table like a displayed specimen. We set up a couple of lamps along with an interactive DNA model on the display. When we finished, it looked halfway convincing. But Dr. Nelson was exasperated.

"That's not hidden," he hissed as Melissa reentered the room.

Tanya assured him, "Plain sight is sometimes the best place to hide something from an eye trained to search."

"Allegory?" he asked her.

"Yes," she replied.

Melissa stepped into the restroom with Tanya to help her get changed. I heard them discuss cleaning off dried blood and Melissa asked, "Oh, my! Is that scar from the injury that killed you?"

My hopes of ever again having a normal conversation vanished that instant. Tanya's voice actually sounded surprised, "Wow. No wonder I died. I didn't realize it would leave a scar."

We men had been nervously silent and, when Tanya's words came through the door, Dr. Nelson nodded and explained to us, as if we had been pondering the biological technicalities, "I was wondering if the cell generator actually differentiated between damaged versus intact cells or if it was a simple growth stimulator. Or if it regrew cells in place, from local stem cells and thus recreated the identical spot." He paused, I suppose to let us catch up, then concluded, "I would think a more involved scanning device would be necessary to sort through damaged cells and remodel them back to their original state. Such a scan-and-clone process would likely result in embryonic cells. Which, of course, would require a much longer healing time."

Dr. Nelson was nodding and we nodded along with him. Suddenly the ladies reentered the room, and Tanya gave me a look that I knew I was supposed to respond to. She remarked, "Not a fan of the reflective stripes, but emerald green is much better."

I nodded and mouthed, "Wow!" and she beamed.

The sound of approaching sirens made me feel suddenly weary. I looked at Melissa and said, "It's time for you to call your dad and have the conversation about coming up here."

The mail clerk gave me a blank stare in return. She glanced at Dr. Nelson, then at Tanya for some help diagnosing what she must have assumed was my amnesia. Thaddeus was the first one to realize her confusion. "Only the five of us have any recollection about your call with your father. In real life, it was undone by our jump back in time."

The young woman nodded to indicate assent and dutifully pulled out her phone. Like a flash of déjà vu, Melissa's call to her father was repeated. Our side of the conversation sounded eerily the same as it had before. The only significant difference was that her father was about one minute away from our location. As the sirens began to turn off, I finally remembered to breathe in. I heard her say, "You're this close, you should come on up, he'll be pleased to meet you. No. Not interrupting at all. Level 3, Room 19. Love you too. See you in a minute."

Melissa dropped her pen-phone into her pocket and looked at Dr. Nelson, beaming. "You're going to get to meet my dad, if we don't have to time jump again." She glanced at me as if to be assured of the schedule. I almost quoted her next phrase with her. "He's on his way up."

There was about a minute and a half of waiting which felt like six weeks. We passed it in uncomfortable silence. I reflected ironically, *We've never actually had time to spare before being confronted. Now we don't know what to do with it.*

We all started at the sharp rap on the door. Melissa pulled it open. "Oh. Hello, Marsha," she said startled, then exclaimed, "Hi, Daddy!" and we could see her give him a hug. "Come on in."

I watched surreptitiously as Marsha glanced around the room with wide eyes and then slowly backed out of the door. I felt a little sorry for her. She would definitely be a candidate for counseling. But I was pretty certain that when I rewound all of the time jumps, she would have no memory of anything confusing and return to her, presumably, shallow existence.

I turned as I was being introduced to Officer Ralph Harris. "This is Dr. Thompson," Melissa said. "He's the inventor of the battery charger."

I was pleased that he was not one of the officers who had arrested me in my initial jump into that time zone. He looked impressed and we shook hands. Melissa moved on. "This is Mr. Willis. He's a patent attorney and does a lot with electronic development."

When they had made the appropriate greetings, she introduced Tanya. "This is Dr. Blake. She's a psychologist and relationship coach. And one of my personal heroes."

Officer Harris shook Tanya's hand and replied, "And, you have the identical gym outfit to the one I got Melissa for Christmas."

Tanya faltered for the first time since I had met her. But Melissa never missed a beat. "Oh, she does! And she has excellent fashion taste."

Then moving to the main event, Melissa said, "This is Dr. Nelson. Henrik. He is the mastermind behind all of the things that happen here at BioChem Labs."

Giving Dr. Nelson a faux stern look, Officer Harris asked, "Okay, young man, what are your intentions with my daughter?"

Naturally, Dr. Nelson did not make the transition to humor. He replied, "Well, sir, I was considering asking her to the Inventors' Congress. But Dr. Blake advised me that dinner and a play, either drama or humor, would be more appropriate for a first date. I've never been on a date before."

The stunned look on the officer's face was priceless. Before he could say anything, Melissa interjected, "Oh, Daddy. Henrik is very literal. He's not going to get your sense of humor."

The officer just nodded awkwardly and took the seat he was offered.

Lieutenant Harris then asked, "Is the receptionist ... okay? I guess I'm trying to politely ask if she has any mental issues. She was adamant, and I won't go into the details, but she claimed that suspicious things were happening here.”

“My professional opinion,” Tanya replied before anyone else could say something inappropriate, “is that she is fine. But she has undoubtedly overheard some bizarre conversations in this room. These guys are certifiable mad scientists. Bless her heart, out of context, some of this stuff could give you nightmares.”

The officer nodded and seemed partially relieved. “She was convinced that people from outer space, or time travelers, had invaded the room. I don’t want to have to arrest her for making a false report, but ...”

Coming to the rescue again, Tanya rolled her eyes and said, “Oh! She overheard some of **that** conversation. Some parts were pretty intense. I can only imagine what’s going through that poor woman’s mind about now.”

“So there was some time travel discussion?” Lt. Harris asked too eagerly.

“Oh, yes,” Dr. Nelson interjected. “We were working out some of the very puzzling aspects of time travel and external navigation and tracking.”

Lt. Harris lit up like a Christmas tree. “So do you think time travel is actually possible?”

It was instantly apparent where Melissa had inherited her intrigue for sci-fi cosplay.

Dr. Nelson replied, “It is undoubtedly possible.”

“Haha! I always knew it had to be possible!” Lt. Harris exclaimed happily as he slid to the edge of the chair. “How long do you suppose it will be before we have actual time travel?”

“Depends on whether you are coming from the future or counting from now,” Dr. Nelson said.

The officer looked confused. I injected, “Within thirty-five years.”

“Oh! Man!” Lt. Harris sounded as giddy as a kid. “Thirty-five years! I’ll be eighty-five. Do you suppose they’ll let regular people ride along?”

Stalling, I hesitantly replied, "Well … there will probably be a lot of bugs to work out."

Officer Harris was in a decidedly good mood as he stood up. "Well. Back to the real world. If you don't intend to lodge a complaint against the secretary, I'm not going to charge her."

"Oh, I believe she acted in good faith," Dr. Nelson replied. Then, in the understatement of all time, he casually added, "She may be a bit more emotionally charged than I am."

Pulling his pen-phone from a shirt pocket, Lt. Harris said, "Here's my personal number. If you ever need anything, feel free to call me direct." They touched pens end-to-end, and I saw a little holographic flash which I took to be the exchange of phone numbers.

After the officer left, Melissa said, "I think Daddy likes you." Dr. Nelson smiled awkwardly. She then showed Dr. Nelson how to save the number into the rapid call format, and how to make sure a call was unstuck. Then, holding the pen about a foot or so from his face, she directed, "Say Daddy's name."

"Daddy's name," Dr. Nelson repeated, and I lost it right there.

Somehow Tanya managed to intervene without laughing, "You need to say his name the way you would address him, or an abbreviation, or nickname. Whatever is the most logical way that you think of him."

"Melissa's father," Dr. Nelson stated.

"Aww," Melissa looked pleased. "Say it again, I wasn't holding the button."

I saw his mouth begin to say, "It again," but he caught himself without coaching, and repeated, "Melissa's father."

Bursting with curiosity, Tanya asked, "Henrik? How did you ever play that role so calmly?"

"Plain sight is sometimes the best place to hide something from an eye trained to search," he repeated her words back verbatim. "Allegorically speaking," he qualified.

The Quest to Find Dr. Khatri

Leaning back in his chair, Dr. Nelson closed his eyes and, for a moment, I was afraid he was taking an afternoon nap. He sat forward abruptly and announced, "The first order of business is to determine if Dr. Khatri is still alive or not. Dr. Thompson, what is your recommendation on how to proceed?"

I had been pondering that exact notion and had a good idea. "I think I should jump back to a moment before their original launch. If I could land within sight of the time box, without being detected, I could observe and jump back quickly."

Thaddeus looked perplexed. "What will you know by that?" he asked.

"If he's not there, he's dead somewhere else. It seems that when you are dead in one time zone, outside of your natural time, you're dead in all time zones," I replied with more certainty than I felt.

Incredulously he blurted, "Then tell me why you are all alive? Because in my time, you would be dead for two hundred years."

"That's chronological time," I explained as if everyone should have learned that in grade school. "We're traveling through time like it's warped sideways. Parallel instead of linear."

Shaking his head, Thaddeus said, "Just tell me where to stand and which button to push. I'm not getting any of that."

Tanya came to me and told Thaddeus, "You give us directions and we'll report back in a flash. Or, actually, sixty-one seconds."

"Nope," I said. "I'm going in alone. You've died in my arms one time too many."

I heard Melissa whisper to Dr. Nelson, "They are so adorable."

"How about some coordinates and directions, Thaddeus? James Bond here needs his assistant," Tanya said as if I had not spoken. She took my arm and I knew there was no reasoning with her.

I tried anyway. "Bond had an Aston Martin and a Walther, looks like I'm not qualified to have a beautiful assistant."

"Goodness! You've invented a time machine! Any fool can get his hands on a stupid car!" Tanya exclaimed in exasperation. "Thaddeus, we need some directions."

The big man helped us locate his shop and we found a perfect landing zone in a supply closet. He then described what Dr. Khatri looked like as if there might be some difficulty differentiating between the giant black-skinned man and a five-and-a-half-foot tall Pakistani.

Melissa squirmed with excitement as we made preparations. She was like a fan at the front row of a concert. I could not help but think she and her dad were very much alike at heart.

"I need both batteries," I muttered, as I tried to give Tanya the slip. But she was wise to my trick and held on tightly.

"We need both batteries," she corrected.

We jumped out and, once again, landed in the impossibly distant future. The supply closet was just as Thaddeus had described, and we stood silently for several minutes. There was no sound at all in the shop except for the distant hum of what I took to be a fan.

Tanya whispered, "This seems like a really bad sign."

I nodded grimly.

"I don't want Dr. Khatri to be dead, but I really am not ready for our time to be done," she whispered again.

I understood. In the back of my mind, I had been wrestling with the inevitable separation we would have to make. Each problem that we solved carried us toward that ultimate moment. And no matter how I rationalized ways for either of us to skip time zones and start over, I was left with the distinct sense that it would be morally wrong. I nodded and, knowing my vulnerability, avoided making eye contact by changing out batteries.

"Kiss me," she whispered. "Here in the glorious future, kiss me."

"I did," I whispered in reply. "I kissed you in the open glen at 2276."

She gave me a cross look and sternly whispered, "That was a ghastly first date. Kiss me while I'm alive."

Looking into her eyes undid me. It was as if the dam restraining all my emotions broached, and all I wanted forever was to hold and be held by her. Nervously I leaned forward and, as our lips almost touched, a door opened. We both started and I instinctively hovered my finger over the button. It was a considerably younger version of Thaddeus. He was slimmer, but still a very large man. And he was distinctly alone.

As Thaddeus worked on what had to be their version of a time travel machine, I wondered if he would make the jump alone. After a minute or two of observation, I gently motioned to my phone and Tanya took my arm. We were both feeling grim and I knew she did not want to have to break the news to Thaddeus any more than I did. As my finger came close to the phone, a toilet flushed somewhere. Miraculously, I stopped before we jumped out. Less than a minute later, a door opened around a corner and we heard the voice of Dr. Khatri.

When he came into sight, his appearance and voice confirmed that he was of Middle Eastern heritage. "Do you think we should pack a lunch?" he asked.

"Is that what you ponder when you're in the bathroom, about to make a historical time travel blastoff?" Thaddeus asked incredulously. "I bet they have food in the future too."

I pressed the button, and Melissa gasped at our sudden appearance. I had forgotten we were that close to her when we had jumped out.

"We saw him," I said.

Thaddeus brightened up noticeably. "I was sitting here remembering. And ... did you get in on the conversation about thinking about lunch in the bathroom?"

That question was like a needle poked into our balloon of suppressed mirth and we both burst out laughing. Melissa jumped up and exclaimed, "Oh! Tell! Do tell!"

We described our jump in full detail minus the personal romantic part. Thaddeus was ecstatic. Dr. Nelson was contemplative. And Melissa, seeming put off a bit, said to me, "You should have given her a kiss in the future. Think of how romantic that would have been."

Tanya surreptitiously poked me in the ribs with her elbow, and I retorted with, "It was only our second date over two-hundred-fifty years. I didn't want to rush things."

"You mean you two aren't married?" Melissa looked genuinely surprised.

"It's a long story," Tanya explained. "Maybe I'll fill you in on it some day."

No, you won't, I thought bitterly, but kept my morose thought to myself.

Impatiently, Thaddeus interrupted, "Dr. Khatri. Finding Dr. Khatri is our task at hand." I suspected he wanted to get back to his family as well, since he was MIA for a couple of months in his chronological time. "He's stuck in a time loop somewhere. How do we find him?"

Everyone looked to me. I looked to Dr. Nelson, who nodded back to me. "He's not in a time loop," I stated without explaining my reservations on the subject. "A continuous loop would need an infinite, or at least extensive, power source. He would hit 2255, instantly reverse, then repeat indefinitely. But, he jumped out of 2276 headed back to 2255 with somewhere between 60% and 80% of the power necessary to get all the way back. My theory is he 'crash landed,' so to speak,

somewhere in between. The problem is, we don't know
if the years or the distance would have been affected
more by the power shortage. Or, since they are
simultaneous impulse modulations affecting both time
and place, there could be an equal split."

Thaddeus nodded. "Simultaneous impulse
modulations," he repeated absently. I knew he was at
least partially with me, but struggling to make the
correlation between time and space frequency
identification.

"It's like the harmonic surge of two dissimilar sine
waves where they intersect. The signature of a given
time is the 'A' wave, and the signature of a given place is
the 'B' wave," I explained.

Thaddeus lit up with comprehension and I knew he had
grasped the concept. I had a rush of satisfaction and
realized then why teachers do what they do.

Tanya just shrugged and I knew that was far away from
her field. Dr. Nelson pondered and I assumed he was
reviewing my technical postulation. Melissa said,
"That's what I was thinking."

Dr. Nelson replied, "Really? Wait. That's humor in the
context of irony. Right?" She beamed at him, and I felt
suddenly guilty knowing that when I made the final
jump into and out of their time zone, they would revert
back to their prior awkward formalities.

I shook off the guilt and proceeded. "I am not sure,
without an infinite power source, how to make a series
of hit-and-miss crisscross searches between the two
times and places. It would be like the game Battleship.
Only, time adds another dimension to the game. The
possible number of options are cubed, in a sense."

"Couldn't we just go back to the moment before Dr.
Khatri and the machine blasted back? Or could we go to
the shop just before we took off in the first place?"
Thaddeus asked.

I took a deep breath and replied, "I don't think so. I
have some doubts."

I looked to Dr. Nelson for some input. He nodded and weighed in. "Since Dr. Khatri is, in reality, lost somewhere outside of his organic time zone, I would have major concerns about intercepting him away from his current reality. There may be a relational conflict which could cause him to … to short out … die, in the process. Life is a tenuous thing, and it likes to be harmoniously attached to its natural parts."

"From my perspective," I rescued the silence that followed his statement, "I think there is a real risk of getting stuck in that time because his actual time signature ended without a definitive modulation. In other words, it was cut short by a power outage."

I looked around the room and jokingly remarked, "Why didn't I concur?"

Tanya laughed, but no one else was nearly old enough to get the reference. We suffered through an uncomfortable silence before Melissa suggested, "It's too bad there's not, like, an internet search engine that could crawl the future and look for references to a time traveler."

Thaddeus and I looked at each other and both said, "Bergman!"

I got up and went to the charger and Thaddeus jumped up beside me. As Tanya came over, I shook my head. "Not this time." She held up my phone. *How does she do that?* I thought. But I did not need an answer, because I knew I must have handed it to her. *I bet she's analyzing my subconscious actions and knows more about me than I do.*

To my surprise, she handed over the phone and, looking down, commented, "Well, if you don't want me along …"

"Wait! Of course I do." The words were scarcely past my lips when she had a grip on my arm. "Yep. I've been played," I remarked wryly. Tanya nodded and Melissa giggled.

Melissa grabbed Dr. Nelson's hand and excitedly asked, "Can we go too?"

"No! No! Please, no," I pleaded. "We're going to land sixteen seconds before a war overruns her hospital. This is not a recreational activity."

"Sixteen seconds?" Thaddeus retorted, concerned.

"Sixteen minutes. Whatever I said, I meant sixteen minutes. There is a war, like exploding bombs, raging outside their walls," I reiterated.

Thaddeus nodded. "It's really bad," he agreed.

"That's not much time to search," Dr. Nelson mused. "Two more people increases the odds of success by 66.7%. It's decided." And like a grade school game, everyone joined arms.

"What have I created here?" I shook my head and muttered under my breath. "Lord, forgive me. She's going to get really sick of me."

I pressed the button.

Bergman

Since I was watching the battery charge indicator, I missed Bergman's expression when we landed. She was about two feet past where she had been when I jumped out. She laughed and shouted over the alarms, "I expected you would be back about now. But I thought you would have better sense than to bring all these people to a war."

Tanya and Melissa were in sudden shock from the flashing lights and screaming sirens. I shook my head in response to Ms. Bergman. "They insisted," was all I could reply.

Dr. Nelson seemed to be completely unaffected by the chaos. I could barely make out his remark. "Peculiar. The lights are pulsing at the rhythm of an at-rest heart, while the sound is at the beat of a panicked, or running, heartbeat. That contradiction seems to generate a sense of emotional unrest."

I shouted over the noise, "We need to search your internet database for a historical reference to a time traveling mad scientist. Dr. Khatri is lost somewhere in time between now and 2255. And somewhere in location between here and Richmond, Virginia. I don't have the technology to track multidimensional irregularities, but I bet the gossip shops of the world have recorded it somewhere."

She nodded as if that was what she had expected. Then pointing to the door, she urged, "Split up into individual rooms and just ask aloud. But be quick. The internet will probably go down when the first mortar hits."

"We have two minutes!" I shouted, and everyone launched into action.

As Tanya passed me, she mused loudly, "You always know the time."

Her words hung in the back of my mind as I asked the wall in Room 199, "Is there still an Area 52 in Nevada?"

Bergman looked amused as the wall replied, "Area 52 is a top secret facility for the military."

"Has there ever been a report, or rumor, of a time traveling machine being taken to Area 52?" I shouted.

"There are 221 results for your requested search. Please clarify with more detail," my wall replied.

"Has there been a reported time travel machine between the years 2255 and 2276, being taken to Area 52?" I yelled again.

"November 27, 22 ..." my wall stopped mid-sentence. Just then the power flicked hard and I knew before I felt the tremor that the first mortar had hit.

We're going to have to jump back two minutes and try again, I thought irritably.

"We've found him!" Tanya exclaimed as everyone piled back into the room. "Actually, Melissa found him. Let's go."

The second mortar hit and dust began to sift through the ceiling joints. "Melissa?" I asked incredulously.

"She's quite an internet guru," Tanya replied at the top of her voice.

Melissa gave me a time and place and I hastily translated the location to coordinates. Looking up, I saw everyone furtively looking at me, and I heard the intercom message like a recurring nightmare, "Last train launch in 9 minutes 48 seconds!"

I made eye contact with Bergman and pointed urgently toward the train station. She pointed stubbornly at my phone. *Is this to be the way we're to remember one another?* I thought, then nodding, I pressed the button.

Our abrupt appearance in the middle of a busy shopping mall created a tremendous stir. I knew I had enough battery to get to 2255, but not enough to get to

2048. People began running in all directions and it only took a few seconds before I heard sirens in the distance. *Ten seconds,* I thought, *These people are quick on the draw.* "Thaddeus. I forgot to ask. Is there a way to charge my batteries in your shop?"

"Yes," he replied as security came running up. Dr. Khatri landed ten feet away, right on schedule. He looked shocked beyond description.

"Touch!" I yelled. As the first security guard on the scene pulled a TASER, I pressed the button. We landed in Dr. Khatri's shop exactly ten minutes before they made their initial launch.

"Yes, sort of, I was going to say!" Thaddeus exclaimed.

"What? My batteries. I might have enough to ... Oh no! Tanya!" I took one quick step back and hit return.

I landed where I had launched from and the pandemonium would have been amusing if I had not seen the TASER dart hit Tanya. I had always been a peaceful, almost pacifistic, person all my life. But in that instant, I was instantly enraged. I charged the officer and crashed my shoulder directly into his chest. With a "whoof," he tumbled down like a bowling pin. I was about to jump on him, but I realized several more officers were rushing to the scene as people screamed all around us.

I hit back 60 seconds and pressed the button on my phone. The officer was drawing his TASER as he ran up. I hit back 30 seconds and, the instant I landed, I kicked a trash can into the path of the rushing officer. It worked perfectly and, tripping hard, he piled up against a support column with a sickening thud. He went down like he had been poleaxed. Ignoring the blood, I grabbed the TASER from the unconscious officer. I turned to Tanya, who was wide-eyed with astonishment. I grabbed her hand and, quickly selecting Dr. Khatri's shop, pressed the button.

The low battery icon flashed. "You've got to be kidding me!" I yelled at the phone.

A quick glance around revealed one option, and I bolted, dragging Tanya into a door that turned out to be a bathroom. "Lean against the door," I shouted, even though she was right there.

Together we leaned against the door and I fumbled to change batteries. The first officer hit the door but did not do much. I knew there would be reinforcements soon. The shouting on the other side of the door seemed really loud, and I realized there was a woman in a stall screaming as well. "How does this stuff happen?" I yelled to no one in particular.

Tanya snapped at the woman in the stall, "Get a grip lady! Zip it!" And amazingly the woman shut up.

There was a much heavier hit against the door, but we barely felt it. I was confused for a second, then Tanya winked at me. I realized she had turned the deadbolt lock.

"I love you," I said.

"I know," she replied. Then she kissed me.

There were more hits from the opposite side of the door and the cursing intensified. A crack developed in the door frame beside the lock's strike plate, and I knew we had only a few seconds. But I was done. I debated about keeping the TASER, but decided to leave it. I tossed it into the trash can, then pressed the button.

Dr. Khatri's Problems

We landed in Dr. Khatri's shop and Dr. Nelson looked up from his watch with a smile. I had selected eleven seconds. I started to say something about the timing when I was struck by a sudden panic. I had not so much as considered that Dr. Nelson and Melissa were time jumping without aging.

Pointing back and forth to Dr. Nelson and Melissa, I gasped, "How are you doing this and not old … or dead?"

He smiled and Melissa excitedly blurted, "He injected us with his magic formula when you and Tanya came here the first time."

I just shook my head. "You know you're surrounded by a bunch of lunatics? Right? We don't have an inkling of what happens in the long run with this stuff!"

"Oh, Dr. Thompson, this is the most excitement I've ever had," she replied dismissively with a nod and a smile.

Tanya took over and told our story from her perspective and I felt compelled to tell of the two prior landings which she, naturally, could not remember. "Wow!" she said, "I'm glad I don't recall getting tazed."

After that, everyone seemed a bit morose as the gravity of our, or my, time jumping mishaps continued to compound in complexity and severity. Out of the blue, Tanya said, "Ask him what happened by the bathroom door." And I could swear she winked at Melissa when she said it.

After being interrogated by Melissa and spilling the whole embarrassing story, Melissa sighed, "You've got to do better than that, Dr. Thompson. She's following you all over the galaxy, or wherever it is we are going. And getting killed, and tazed, and everything, just to be with you a few minutes longer. You've got to do better."

After taking my berating from the mailroom girl, I looked to Thaddeus. "Charger?"

With a determined sigh, he nodded and began rummaging through shelves of miscellaneous electrical components. "We'll need to make a simple step transformer," he replied.

"You don't have a standard toaster oven, charge-all device?" I asked disbelievingly.

He looked pained and admitted, "We have a Focal Impulse Charging lamp in the office. It's not like the hospital that had them everywhere. Just one fixture. They must have gotten a lot cheaper in the future. But ... the office is sort of off-limits at the moment."

"Off-limits?" I asked, "From your own office?"

"His office," Thaddeus indicated Dr. Khatri. "The police are still in there."

My heart sank. "Now I wish I had held onto that TASER," I muttered. "Are they looking for the time travel device?" I cautiously asked.

Dr. Khatri dejectedly sat down on a wooden crate. "Tax evasion," he admitted.

I looked around the room at each person there. Tanya gently rubbed my shoulder and asked, "What now?"

Looking at the floor in despair, I tried to think of something clever to say, but drew a blank. Then I heard, "This is Dr. Jalal Khatri. I will meet you at the Office of Revenue and Taxation in forty-five minutes. I will have all of my tax papers with me. The papers you are seeking are not in my office. Your police buffoons are wasting their time." There was a pause and he said, "Thank you very much. I will see you there."

Looking through the lattice window covering, Thaddeus announced, "The police are leaving the office."

"Dr. Khatri," Melissa gasped, "You're turning yourself in, just to save us?"

Without hesitation he replied, "To save you: Yes. Turning myself in: No. The police are gullible dolts. We have played this cat-and-mouse game for over a decade. I refuse to pay taxes to a non-representative government, run by idiot bullies. You had better get those batteries charged, Thaddeus. They need to go home, and we need to move to the farm."

Thaddeus raced off to the office, and Melissa whispered to Dr. Nelson, "This is such a better date than dinner and a play." He smiled in response, but I suspected there were much deeper thoughts brewing in his head than she could fathom. Even Tanya was subdued.

Thaddeus rushed into the shop and practically tossed the batteries into my hands. "Go. Now!" he snapped. "Hurry!"

As I hurriedly installed a battery into my phone, Melissa asked the question I did not want to. "What's the matter now?"

"The Sicilians are here," he hissed as he barricaded heavy items in front of the door. "They're going to the office first. Dr. Khatri, how is our battery charge?"

"I thought you plugged it in," Khatri blurted.

"When have I had time for that?" Thaddeus snapped as he raced to connect the time travel box to power. "It's going to need at least thirty minutes to recharge long enough to jump back 8 hours to fully charge for a real jump out," he moaned.

"Are they going to try to kill you?" Melissa asked nervously.

"They're gonna do more than try," Thaddeus muttered.

"Dr. Thompson will do something clever to save you," Melissa replied with unwavering certainty.

"Are they after the time machine?" Dr. Nelson asked.

"They financed the development, and it's taken too long to get a payback from it. Today is the day they will kill us," Dr. Khatri sounded resolved as he watched the charge indicator blink. There was no possible way the barricade could hold up long enough for the batteries to get charged.

My mind was numb with chagrin. I had a sudden realization that I was looking at one of my first iterations for a time travel device. *This is the actual device made from drawings I worked up for my senior science fair project!* I thought. *Where were those drawings stored? In Dad's safe? That must have been the case. I've got to destroy those drawings and notes when I jump back there. This is totally out of hand.*

Out loud, I laughed, "I got disqualified at the science fair for this project. The judges criticized me for trying to pass science fiction for science."

Dr. Nelson cheerfully replied, "Well, you can get the last laugh on them. There is something profoundly satisfying about developing an idea that is purported to be impossible."

I did not feel particularly vindicated at that moment. I had the sickening sense that those judges may have been trying to dissuade me from making something that would prove to be incredibly dangerous.

"These guys, the Sicilians. Are they the reason you jumped to 2276?" I asked. Then without waiting for an answer, I finished the mystery. "You were jumping to a safe house, to the farm. Pan-dimensional hide and seek."

Dr. Khatri nodded and Thaddeus shrugged and I knew he was afraid. "Jump now," Thaddeus insisted.

"That was actually a mathematically brilliant idea," Dr. Nelson interjected. "The odds of being found, as we have discovered, are exponentially compounded when the dimension of time is inserted into the equation as a variable."

"True. Now, let's go," I ordered, but no one moved.

"Is there nothing we can do to help them?" Melissa asked.

"There's a revolution going on in 2276," I reminded them.

Suddenly Dr. Khatri noticed that Thaddeus had not returned to his chronological age. "Why are you still old?" he blurted.

"We're a few minutes away from getting rubbed out by the mob, and you want to ask about petty stuff?" Thaddeus snapped. "These people helped save you. And if they don't get out of here, they're going to die too. And you know it."

Dr. Khatri swept his hand in my direction and retorted, "He's already working on a plan."

The truth was, I had been working out a plan, and at that moment, I pressed the button.

I landed in the bathroom back at the mall with the police battering against the door. It had only been a half minute since Tanya and I had left, but the door was about to give way when I grabbed the TASER out of the trash can. The mind can move at an incredible pace, and I wondered at the conversation that was taking place in my absence. *Did he ditch us here? Is this the place we all die? Or perhaps Dr. Nelson was educating Dr. Khatri on the side effects of the cell serum.* I selected my jump back default and timed the door battering. They were striking every six seconds. As soon as there was a solid hit, I waited about three seconds, then gently unlocked the deadbolt. About three seconds after that I pressed the jump button.

I heard it, but sadly missed the show, when the police slammed against that door. I imagined they crashed through with some ferocity. I was laughing when I landed in Dr. Khatri's shop sixty-one seconds after I had jumped out.

"Nothing is funny here!" Tanya exclaimed hotly as she wrapped her arms around me. "Why did you leave me behind?"

I waved the TASER behind her back. "Someone unbolted that door the police were battering. I bet it was quite the spectacle when they flew through without any resistance."

"Chad. Our time together is limited. It's so … limited. Please don't leave me behind again, until it has to be so." Her plea made a lump form in my throat. I nodded in agreement and she squeezed me closer. I tried not to think about our time ending.

"They're coming," Thaddeus said.

I tossed him the TASER. "These have a feature on them that is called a 'walker.' If you can figure out how to drive it, you can hijack one of the bad guys and make him fight the others," I instructed, but added, "At least I think it can be worked that way."

"There are twelve of them," he said.

"Twelve!" Melissa gasped.

"They can be operated independently, or in parallel, but there is only one control. So they'll all do the same thing. It's a lot like playing a game," Thaddeus explained.

"Twelve bad guys?" Melissa reiterated.

"Darts. Twelve TASER darts. Three bad guys," he replied. Someone slammed against the shop door. He looked at me and shrugged, "I wrote the patent for the walker."

"Nice," I replied.

"You have the control?" he asked.

"What?" I gasped at my omission.

"Too bad," Thaddeus mused. It was obvious that his attention was on the opposite side of the door. Absently he remarked, "The darts' default setting is 'Demobilize.' It'll take 'em down. It's like having your insides boiled alive."

There was some more banging and some muffled cursing at the shop door. The pile of stuff blocking the door shifted, and I grinned at the big man. There was a gleam in his eyes that made me glad I was not on the other side of that door. "This is where we jump out. Good luck, my friend," I said with a salute.

Just then a bullet shattered through the small window on the door. "Whoa! Let's go!" I shouted. And Melissa and Dr. Nelson scrambled to me. Tanya had not let go. I selected Dr. Nelson's office, and pressed the button.

The instant we landed, Dr. Nelson said, "I would have loved to see that TASER in action."

I shook my head, remembering Thaddeus taking multiple hits from one at the train station in Bergman's hospital. I also remembered my own experience on the business end of one of those darts. "No," I shook my head. "No, you probably wouldn't."

Infinite Life

We all settled in at Dr. Nelson's office, and Tanya would not let go of my arm. The reality was, I did not want her to. But I knew the next logical step was for me to jump back home with Farren's remains, then begin undoing all my prior jumps. I said as much to Dr. Nelson, and Melissa seemed perplexed.

"You mean being a time jumper doesn't give you an infinite life span?" she asked.

I tried to think of where to start explaining, but Dr. Nelson beat me to it. "No," he replied, "life has a beginning and an end and the biological reality relentlessly moves us toward death. When a unique cell definition is created, that is, when there is a conception, the cellular encoding begins its own timer. It's like a sand glass. The grains of sand fall into the lower chamber and no amount of coaxing can make them go back up. Eventually all of the grains of sand fall, and it is done. Death is a powerful and irreversible end. Everything we do medically to extend life only affects external factors that are seeking to prematurely terminate that life."

He looked at Melissa and asked, "Is this making any sense? Or am I overanswering the question?"

Melissa's eyes briefly flicked toward Tanya and me. "It's not making a lot of sense, but I like hearing you explain it," she replied.

"Is the metaphor working?" he asked.

"That's about the only part I understand," she admitted, then asked, "So how did we stay young with your magic serum? Will we age again some day?"

"The cell-encoder serum simply tricks the cell's signaling mechanism into believing that time is not passing. That is a temporary state and it will wear off, and the chronological age will again be evident. Dr. Thompson's time signature device does much the same thing, only it resets the 'now' signal to a different time reality. But the meter of life never stops." Dr. Nelson had summarized a lot of technology into a succinct description.

Melissa was thinking pretty hard about what Dr. Nelson had said. At length, she asked, "How were you able to bring Tanya back to life?"

Pursing his lips, Dr. Nelson explained, "There was a lot of technology used to signal the cells that were not dead, to reverse the death trigger mechanism. And, the truth is, we don't really know what happened there. I'm not entirely sure we didn't witness a miracle, like that lady from Tijuana said."

"How does Dr. Thompson remaking his visits fix all the problems that have happened?" Melissa asked, and I began to suspect she was stalling for time.

Dr. Nelson gave me the nod, so I began, "I don't exactly know how things are going to play out. But, when I undo a jump, I land a few seconds before the prior jump, then I jump out, leaving a vacuum of the previous experience. Like when Tanya was tazed. I jumped back a minute and she had no recollection of it, because it didn't actually happen. Or it un-happened, if you can get your mind around that kind of reality. That's because I intercepted the event. Then I jumped back another half minute and she, nor the officer, nor anyone else there, had any recollection of the other jumps. Basically it unmade the event. I don't know how far that reaches. I also have had to be careful to not unmake a solution and reignite a problem. Unfortunately, I will not be able to resolve the war of 2276. Farren was part of that and … at least I think I would need him to jump in and out to undo his part of that reality as well."

"What happens to us?" Melissa's tone told me she knew the truth.

I nodded. "I'm sorry. I don't know any way around it."

"Could we jump back with you so we would still be ...?" She cut off her sentence for lack of a good definition.

"That would simply remake the event, not unmake it," I explained, knowing I was oversimplifying it.

"How much more time can we take?" Melissa sounded desperate.

Tanya had found her pen-phone on the desk just then, and checked her messages. "Oh, my!" she whispered. "I have over three hundred messages. It's been less than twenty-four hours." She listened to several in a row and became somber. With quavering voice she whispered, "You've got to go. They've put a shoot-to-kill warrant out for you." Then she began to weep.

I took Tanya's hand and glanced at Dr. Nelson, as if I would get good relationship advice from him. Reassuringly I said, "They don't know where I am. So we've got a little time yet."

Just then Melissa got an incoming call. "Hi, Daddy," she answered. Instantly, the cold reality of the situation hit me. When Tanya had activated her phone, it had signaled law enforcement, and given away our location.

I could have predicted Melissa's next words. "Yes. She's here. Abducted by Dr. Thompson? No, she's fine. Yes ... A dangerous escaped inmate?"

I stood up with the sickening resignation that there were no other options. My time was up. "I am so sorry," I whispered to Tanya as I pulled her to her feet. "I have been trying to get as much time as I could with you .... I'm sorry."

I pulled her close for a final, and real, kiss. I was suddenly nervous and involuntarily closed my eyes. I could sense her presence as we gently moved closer together and all other sensation faded into the distance. As our lips met, Dr. Nelson casually mentioned, "That seems too bad. I think I've figured out how to resuscitate your friend Farren. But I estimate we would need another ten minutes."

It was like falling through ice into the bitter waters of a lake. Her eyes opened with a flash of annoyance and, in frustration, she whispered, "Can we go someplace private for one real kiss?"

I let go of her and backed away. Stepping to Dr. Nelson, the distant sound of sirens made the bad news worse. "Let go of her hand," I ordered. He released Melissa, who was still on the phone with her father. The look of concern on her face was borderline panic. I touched Dr. Nelson and pressed back 120 seconds. We landed and both of the ladies jumped, because, it appeared that I had teleported across the room.

Tanya was mid-reach for her phone and I grabbed her hand. "No! You need to leave that off." Then I quickly filled them in on what had transpired.

Wide-eyed, Melissa asked, "So we have less than two minutes?"

"I don't know how much time we have. If they don't receive the alert from Tanya's phone, it may take a while for the abducted and wanted bulletins to be noticed by anyone not directly on the case." Then turning to Dr. Nelson, I said, "Shoot."

He looked startled for a second, and I had a momentary panic that he had forgotten the plan. Melissa whispered, "It's a figure of speech that means it's your turn to say something important."

He nodded, then explained, "Here is my postulation. If you were to take the remains of Farren to the time of his conception, and inject a stem cell growth hormone into the core of the bones ..."

"Stop!" I held up my hand as I interrupted. "Did you actually say take his bones back to the time of his conception?"

Dr. Nelson nodded. I tried to formulate a sentence that conveyed how utterly impossible and ridiculous that sounded. Finally I blurted, "What? I suppose I'm going to go to his parents and quiz them about that?"

"No. We'll cover that," he replied, unfazed. "Inject the hormone into the core and then travel to his organic time zone. If my understanding of how you shift the frequency of your cells to a different time reality is correct, then your cells are actually responding by becoming their own biological potential. So, in fact, Melissa, you were not far from the truth when you asked if time travel could give one infinite life. It's by no means infinite, but it is fulfillment of all the potential years encoded into one's DNA."

I stared at the mad scientist like a cow stares at a post. Finally I managed, "Where do I find some of this stem cell stuff to inject?"

"Well, that's going to be tricky because it doesn't exist yet. But, I have an experimental batch," was the reply I had been dreading. "I wish we had time to jump a couple of years into the future to see how the testing had worked. But with your propensity for getting locked up or shot at, I don't believe we should take that chance."

"So, how do we determine his time of conception? Without anything really embarrassing, please," I asked.

"That's simple," he stated. "Just go back to 268 days prior to his birthday. Then jump back by half day increments until his remains vanish. Then jump forward to undo the last jump. I think that will get you close enough to the point when his DNA was defined for the cells to respond properly."

I felt a little sick to my stomach. Sitting down, I asked, "What happens if his remains vanish but don't rematerialize when I jump that half day forward?"

Dr. Nelson leaned back in his chair and took a deep breath before he replied, "Regrettably, I don't have an answer for that."

"Is there any other possible option?" I asked. I felt like addressing him as Dr. Frankenstein.

"You could leave him dead," he replied. "And Bergman's world in a full-blown war. That part is assuming it was really you, or your device, that the hostiles in that time were after."

I looked at the floor in despair. There was no doubt it was my phone they were after, and I knew I had to try to fix it. Tanya rubbed my shoulders again, and I could not help thinking how nice life would be shared with her. "We can do it," she whispered.

"All right," I said as I stood up. "Let's do this thing."

Dr. Nelson held up his index finger and added, "Oh. And you'll need to borrow one of those cell mender blow guns from Bergman too."

My shoulders slumped. "She's going to get really sick of me showing up," I muttered. "Maybe I'll jump to the morgue and grab the cell mender there before I got it last time."

Then realizing my error, I said, "I can't pick it up there. It won't be there when I needed it for Tanya. I can't undo that."

Dr. Nelson remarked, "You have to go chronologically after our last visit."

"Bergman's going to miss the train," I countered.

"If you go before that, you risk unfinding Dr. Khatri," Dr. Nelson rejoined.

"Is it fair to let Bergman die to save Farren?" I asked. That moral dichotomy kept surfacing, and it was troubling me deeply.

Dubiously, Tanya asked, "The cell healing gun is in Room 199, right? Can we jump in there right after Bergman left, and then jump back out, without engaging her? That won't change the trajectory of history with Dr. Khatri that's already happened. Right?"

"I think that might work," I replied, equally dubiously, then looked to Dr. Nelson for a rebuttal.

Dr. Nelson put his hands together and tapped his index fingers together slowly, and I knew he was processing, and it was probably more than I could comprehend. At length, he responded, "If you can pull off your snatch-and-grab mission as Dr. Blake has proposed, and no other human was encountered, I believe that you can eavesdrop on history, such as it is, without interrupting it." The look on his face told me that he was still processing, and he added, "We're really starting to split hairs on the outer rim of this uncharted territory. But I think that has the greatest probability of successfully not disrupting the search for Dr. Khatri, and not putting Bergman into any further risk of missing the train, and retrieving the device that we need to attempt to resuscitate Farren."

Tanya handed me my phone. I set the landing time and the jump-back time. "We'll be back in 11 seconds," I said. Tanya had not let go of me, and I pressed the jump button.

It doesn't matter how many times you suddenly arrive into a battle zone, the shrieking sirens, the shaking building, the dust falling from the ceiling, the chaotic flashing lights, and the sounds of panicking people fleeing are unnerving. It was even more unnerving to think that if everything went perfectly as planned, I still had to jump back in here one more time to return that stupid cell healer. I had one of those random irrelevant thoughts: *I wonder if I checked out a library book, what the 250-year fine would be?* Tanya interrupted my reverie and asked, "Is this what we're looking for?" I nodded, and hit the jump button to go back.

As programmed, we landed 11 seconds after we had left. Within a second, Melissa got an incoming call. "Oh, no," I moaned. "I thought we were going to have more time than this."

She answered. "Hi, Daddy. Umm, she's fine."

I began to key another jump. "I'm running out of options," I muttered irritably as I tried to identify a good time to land.

Melissa's conversation continued. "She should be OK there. There's no way in or out without being screened, and the security is pretty tight. Yes, they scan for all that stuff there, and she's had all her immunizations. But I'll be sure to have her checked out at the clinic after work this evening. OK, love you. Bye bye." Melissa looked up from her private conversation and, in perplexity, commented, "Seems like every few months, there's another virus going around that's worse than any other that's ever been. McKenna doesn't ever seem to get any of the nasty bugs, but I'm paranoid, so I get her vaccinated. But I'm starting to wonder if those medicine companies are inventing those viruses, just to drum up business."

Dr. Nelson nodded. "Yes, and they're poorly-engineered viruses as well. They mutate rapidly but, on the positive side, they leave in their wake a trail of antibodies so, in effect, they're self-destructive in the long run. Dark side of the industry, but a common practice. Part of the reason I left the mainstream industry and started my own foundation."

My respect for Dr. Nelson soared to a whole new level. I had the private suspicion that if he decided to take over the world single-handedly, he probably could.

"Do we have to be in the accurate location for conception?" I asked hesitantly.

Dr. Nelson replied, "No, assuming my understanding of your field is accurate. There is an axis about which two frequency signatures intersect. One of these signatures defines the individual's DNA at a given time, and the other defines the individual's DNA at a given place. Is that correct?"

I nodded. Dr. Nelson continued, "Since each of those frequency signatures is autonomous, the place is essentially irrelevant to our experiment today."

I wondered if everything was a laboratory experiment in his mind. "Farren's birthday was January 18, 1981." I did a calendar calculation on my phone, and muttered to myself, "This is really, really weird. Intrusive weird. Let's see, 268 days, that would be ... April 26, 1980. I really feel like I'm invading into some pretty personal stuff here."

Dr. Nelson commented, "It's all just algorithms and biology, Dr. Thompson."

That seemed to dehumanize it a bit, but it made it easier to focus on the work without feeling embarrassed.

"Next question ..." I was pretty concerned about this next part. "Are we going to need to, like, bottle-feed him? And, you know, diapers?"

"No. You're re-stimulating the life in the cells, and then simply translating that life to a different time. The entirety of the energy necessary to accomplish that is inside those batteries. They made you old, and they made you young. They'll do the same for him, in the appropriate chronological context."

Out of the blue, Melissa asked, "Tanya, did you highlight your hair?"

"No-o-o," Tanya replied.

Dr. Nelson grabbed his bio kit. "Aha, the serum is beginning to wear off. We need to do bio's."

I realized just then that the ache in my shoulder had been slowly increasing.

Dr. Nelson quickly took bio samples from us and ran his tests. "By my calculation, you should have two more chronological hours, but it will progressively wear off, so you need to hurry."

I keyed in the time, and pondered a location where I thought we would be able to work in privacy. I selected the treehouse at my grandparent's farm. My dad had made it when he was a teen. It was one place that I knew people did not just happen to run across. They had to be on their way to the treehouse to find it.

Dr. Nelson opened the wire mesh, and I was really hoping that would not come with us when we made the jump. We transferred Farren's remains into a blanket, and rolled it all up like a giant burrito.

The syringe with the cell-cloning serum was much larger than I had expected. Dr. Nelson also gave me an electronic microscope and a quick tutorial on how to use it. He quickly showed me the difference between dormant stem cells and multiplying stem cells, and what I would be looking for when we did the procedure on Farren.

When we had everything gathered together, Tanya touched me and Farren's remains and, just as I heard Melissa say, "Good luck!" I pressed the button.

I immediately felt younger. And I was shocked to see that Tanya looked like a teenager. Tanya and I looked at each other, and with a giggle, Tanya said, "We'd better hurry. I won't be born for over four years yet."

"Yeah, I'm about a year-and-a-half out myself," I said, afraid my voice would start cracking. I really did not want to have to go through puberty a second time, and especially not backward. "This feels like Novocaine wearing off. It's still there, but not quite all the way, and there's no good way to describe the sensation."

Tanya replied, "Yeah, let's hurry, so we at least have a chance to try to describe it."

Just then, I had a mini panic attack, because the blanket was empty. "Oh, no!" I whispered. "Farren's remains didn't jump with us." I don't know why I whispered, I just felt we needed to be secretive. My judgment might have been affected by my sudden regression back to my adolescence.

Tanya whispered in reply, "Wait, no, we're supposed to jump in small increments until he re-materializes."

I set for us to jump ahead by 12 hours. We landed, and there was still nothing in the blanket. Tanya hissed, "Are you sure you did the math right?"

I retorted, "Dr. Nelson would have caught it if I had done it wrong."

"He's not infallible," she argued.

I could not think of an appropriate rebuttal, so I grabbed her hand and jumped ahead another 12 hours.

The bones were there. "It worked!" Tanya stage-whispered excitedly.

I never imagined that I would be so happy to find a pile of bones. My next moment of panic was a horrible fear that we needed to arrange the bones into their appropriate places. I began to assemble the skeleton, but Tanya urged, "Just make 'em touch." I began to inject the clone serum into all of the major bones, and I repeated the process until the syringe was empty. Tanya turned on the cell-growth stimulator, and began to wave it over the pile of bones. It could have been a hilarious practical joke except for the gravity of the situation. I began to study the cells with the microscope, and Tanya crowded close to see the screen as well. After about 30 seconds of nothing, I was about to declare our experiment a failure, when the first hint of cell multiplication showed up. It was not as clear as it had been on Dr. Nelson's illustration, and I strained my eyes trying to actually see a single cell split into two, but it seemed like I blinked at the wrong instant every time. Then suddenly I realized that there were many more cells than when we had begun watching. Excitedly I whispered, "I think it's working!"

"How long do you suppose we should give it?" Tanya whispered back.

A sound came wafting up to us. "I built this when I was a sophomore in high school," I heard a voice say. And I realized that it was the voice of my father. I looked through a space in the planking. His resemblance to me was uncanny.

Tanya whispered, "She looks just like you. She must be your mom." I looked at Tanya and said, "This is going to be really awkward, since I'm not born yet."

I did a quick date calculation and realized that I had heard the story about this event numerous times while growing up. My parents had just gotten back from their honeymoon, and my mom had insisted that my dad show her his beloved treehouse, of which she had heard so much about. Her foot had slipped and she had fallen while climbing up the ladder. Her wrist was broken badly and required a pretty involved surgery that included several pins and screws.

As my parents were rapidly approaching the ladder to the treehouse, I quickly whispered the story to Tanya. We both looked at the cell-multiplier device. We obviously had the same thought at the same time. I experienced a new low in my time-travel escapades. I knew my parents would have a heart attack if they met their son before his time, and it would have been impossible to convince them that I was time traveling. We hastily gathered our stuff, and jumped back to Dr. Nelson's office, leaving my own mother to suffer an injury that I could have easily healed in minutes.

I crashed to the floor in Dr. Nelson's office, because Farren was a lot heavier than his dry bones had been. I think we all freaked out there for a few minutes when we realized Farren was indeed alive and thrashing around inside that blanket. I got his head uncovered, and he looked around the room in astonishment. Finally he focused on me. "Wow, you've really turned gray," he said. I didn't want to point out to him that he was in his late sixties. I decided he would figure that out soon enough. I looked at Dr. Nelson and said, "Tanya and I could both feel ourselves de-aging back there. We've got to hurry. We need some clothes for Farren. And he needs to be injected so we can jump to 2276."

Dr. Nelson pointed to the bathroom and said, "I have a closet full of clothing in there." I must have given Dr. Nelson a really funny look, because he added, "I spend two-thirds of my waking hours here. So it only makes sense that two-thirds of my wardrobe is here."

I rushed Farren into the bathroom and practically threw clothes at him. Everything in the closet was the same color, so the choices were easy. He hurriedly dressed as I explained to him what had happened through our misadventures of time travel. He just kept shaking his head and saying, "Oh, my! Oh, my!"

I knew I had not given him a fair rundown, because we simply did not have enough time. I also was aware that we had chronologically used up about 8 minutes of Dr. Nelson's estimated 10-minute window. Dr. Nelson came in with the serum, and said, "I'm sorry that we don't have time to do bio's, but we need to jump back to your organic time zone to inject, because you guys are going to have to make a hasty retreat out of here once you get back from 2276."

"I'll do it," Tanya yelled from the other room.

Farren asked, "Who is she?"

I was surprised to hear myself say, "My girlfriend, Tanya."

Then Farren asked, "And who is this doctor?"

I replied, "This is Dr. Nelson. The mad scientist. The savant genius that I told you about."

"Uh huh," Farren mumbled.

Tanya rapped on the bathroom door. "Ready or not, we've got to go. Melissa's phone just got an alert that I've been abducted by a hostile inmate. It's a missing person report, and so far her father hasn't called her."

Dr. Nelson instructed Tanya, "This is a micro-dose that, by my calculation, is just enough, so that the effects of this should wear off within a few minutes of yours and Chad's."

"I've got a problem," I declared. Everyone looked at me with the question in their eyes. "I've run out of places to land us."

"I'm dead for a few days, and you've got trouble in every time zone?" Farren asked in exasperation.

"In my defense, you were dead for a couple hundred years," I retorted irritably. My nerves were too jangled at that point to be amused by any diversion.

Farren asked, "Can't we just go to my place?"

I replied, "FBI, CIA, local police. It's a pretty busy place about now."

"We could go to my place," Tanya offered.

I was instantly electrified by the idea that, though Tanya would forget me, I would have a way to contact her, once everything was settled back into its right position. Just as quickly, I had a sudden sense of certain dismay, realizing that there was no way that I could tell her that we had been time traveling together and had fallen in love. I handed her my phone with the app open, and I whispered, even though everyone else could hear, "You know you won't remember me."

She put her finger to my lips, and whispered back, "Let's not live that heartache until we have to."

In chronological time, I figured that would take place in about five more minutes. A lump formed in my throat and I could not reply.

I was surprised to see that, at that time, Tanya lived in Beaumont, Texas. I tried to fill in Farren about the battery situation as he loaded the battery into his phone. But it was obvious that he was overwhelmed by everything that was happening and it was not sinking in.

I gave up on the lesson and instructed him to save the current location and set the return time for 11 seconds. He gave me a quizzical look. I nodded toward Dr. Nelson and said, "He's really big on prime numbers."

I was pretty sure Farren got that. "OK," was all he replied as he made the entry.

The three of us touched, and I pushed the button for the jump.

Beaumont

We landed in Tanya's apartment and were immediately overwhelmed by sweltering muggy air. It smelled terrible. "Oh, my goodness!" she gasped. "The week from Beelzubub. I didn't remember this date, but the power was out for, like, five days after a hurricane. That's when I decided I had to move out of Beaumont."

Tanya quickly injected Farren and I mused aloud, "I hope this stuff isn't bothered by the heat." She gave me a concerned glance, but I could only shrug. "I don't know. We'll find out in a second here," I replied to the unasked question in her eyes.

We were all sweating profusely, so to initiate some levity, I asked with mock sincerity, "Dr. Helton, are you ready to become a time lord? Because you're about to initiate your first time jump in which you don't die."

We all touched, and he was grinning like a monkey when he touched that button.

"That was an absolute rush!" Farren exclaimed when we touched down in Dr. Nelson's office.

"Don't get used to it," I remarked, "because when we unwind this time bomb, we've got to destroy these machines."

"Quickly now," Dr. Nelson said. "The wire mesh and the cell multiplier need to go back to Bergman's hospital." We threw our phones in the charger and, in about 15 seconds, we were ready to go again.

Farren said, "I like that machine. It's pure genius."

Tanya beamed. And I just replied, "You're welcome."

I pointed at Farren and said, "Stand by. We'll be back in 11."

"I don't get to come with?" Farren asked in dismay.

"Why does everybody want to go with me into the war zone?" I didn't wait for an answer, but pressed the jump button. I had already programmed the in and the out. We landed in the chaos of the hospital building being shelled. Tanya tossed aside the items that belonged in that time zone and just then, a slab of concrete broke off from directly over us. Instinctively I shoved Tanya away.

I woke up, and the only lights were the flashing lights of the alarm. I could barely make out that Tanya was hovering over me with the cell multiplier pointing at my head. I could feel hot water dripping, which I presumed was from a broken water line. It turned out to be Tanya's tears. She said, "We need to go. I thought I'd lost you there for a while."

I asked, "What happened to the lights?"

She replied, "The power's been out for about 15 minutes."

I jumped up the best I could manage, choking in all the dust that was in the air. "Are we charged?"

"We're at 100%," Tanya said, and handed me my phone.

We jumped out and landed in Dr. Nelson's office, and both Melissa and Farren looked aghast when they saw me. Dr. Nelson made the analysis. "Judging by the blood stains, you lost about three pints."

I nodded, but just mumbled, "Yeah, I don't remember any of that." Then asked, "What's the status of our emergency alert here?"

Melissa replied, "No news is good news."

"Okay, good," I responded. "Now we need to jump in with your phone. Let's just arbitrarily pick 15 seconds before you landed. And then we'll jump back out with my phone. And we'll be back here in 11 seconds. And if all of our theories are correct, and all the stars line up, we might actually successfully unmake the history that we've messed up."

Farren asked, "Why are we jumping in on one phone and out on the other?"

"Battery life," I oversimplified as I pulled my phone from the charger. I knew I didn't have time for a complete explanation. Tanya and I were both showing a few more gray hairs. "Let's jump," I said. At that instant, Melissa got the call we had all been dreading.

"Hi, Daddy," she said.

I pointed to Farren's phone and said, "Jump." And he pressed the button.

We landed on the opposite side of the serene glen in the woods. I again marveled that it was the same place in which Independence Hall had stood in our days. In amazement, Farren opened his mouth to make a comment, but I motioned for silence. We waited for 20 seconds and just then I spotted two men from the white militia. They were hunkered down behind some shrubbery, peering into the forest with their backs to us. Our time had passed and, as one of them began to turn around, I pressed the jump button.

We landed, and I had a sense of exhilaration. "It worked!" I exclaimed. "At least, I think we made it work!"

Dr. Nelson responded, "It's unfortunate that we don't have a way of verifying that scientifically without the risks associated with reentry."

I could hear Melissa in urgent conversation with her father. And I tossed our phones into the charger for the last time. That was oddly poignant.

I told Dr. Nelson, "I can't think of any safe way to jump into that hospital. If they're still at war, it's too dangerous, and if they're not, I'll have stirred up the whole pot again."

He said, "If you can find it in your scientific ethic to jump back to this time and be seen by me, I'd be very interested in speaking with you if I remember any of this." He stopped, and then recanted, "Although, that would probably be too risky." We could hear the sirens in the background.

I tossed Farren his phone, and told him, "Jump back home the morning you disappeared. Get a shower, go to work, pretend everything is normal. As far as I know, that undoes everything on your side."

He asked, "What about you?"

I said, "I'm going to do the same. But I've got a little unfinished business here."

Farren jumped out, and I was startled at the abruptness of his disappearance. *It's no wonder*, I thought, *that people get riled up about that.* I shook Dr. Nelson's hand. "It's been a privilege," I said. I interrupted Melissa's conversation with her dad, knowing that I was about to completely undo it anyway. "Melissa, it's been a pleasure meeting you. Say 'Hi!' to your dad for me. It's okay to tell him the truth about what is going on here." She looked startled, and I could hear him asking what was going on. The sirens were getting closer and I knew that the time was about up. I waved and remarked, "I've got to be going home now."

I took Tanya's hand, and we stepped out into the hallway. I took her into my arms, and realized that the cell serum had completely worn off. We were senior citizens.

Through tears, she said, "I guess we've gotten to grow old together. We've died in each other's arms. We brought Farren from embryo to adulthood. And we've seen the world together. Which is more than a lot of people get to experience. But … I wish, more than anything else in the world, that I could remember you after this."

I just shook my head, and replied, "I wish I could forget." She nodded, and I knew she understood. I said, "One proper kiss." And there in the hallway of BioChem Laboratories, we kissed for real.

I may have actually lost track of time in that experience, because when I looked up, an aghast Eyelash Marsha was staring at us with an expression of consternation. I knew it was really mischievous of me. I waved at her and said, "Goodbye, Marsha."

When I stepped back from Tanya, I was instantly overwhelmed by the sensation of imminent loss. I had intended to say something witty, but in that moment I was unable to speak. In fact, my vision blurred so badly, I could hardly see. Through the fog in my eyes, I could see tears streaming freely down Tanya's cheeks.

The best I could do was mouth the words, "I love you," then I pressed the jump. It felt like emotional suicide.

I landed in the EXL hallway, just outside of where my office had been all those years before. I was pretty sure I was outside the view of any security camera in that spot. But I still could not see anything for my tears. I hoped my choice was a good one.

It was 15 seconds prior to my first arrival into 2048, and I was very relieved that no one was in the hallway. I waited for 20 seconds to cross the history threshold, then pressed for the jump home, and landed in my own bathroom.

I leaned heavily against the counter for a few minutes to force myself to accept the grim new reality. *It's done. History unmade. As of now, she never met you,* I told myself. *Now you've got to suck it up and deal with it.*

I felt sick to my stomach, but looking at the time, I knew I needed to get moving. *I need a shower,* I thought, *and I've got to burn these blood-stained clothes.*

No Place Like Home

My mind raced through the chaotic events of what had been roughly 72 hours of my chronological life. It is difficult, if not impossible, to sort such things into order when one is pondering 250 years of experiences that have already taken place later in the same day. It was like trying to write a report while only using the letters in alphabetical order. My head hurt.

Counseling was out of the question. I knew I could never actually speak about my experiences to anyone, or I would find myself in a straight jacket – again! There had been enough of that already.

Besides the irreconcilable paradox of non-chronological experiences, I had several other layers of conflict in my mind. First, but by no means least, was the actual scientific question of *Did I actually affect history, or was the outcome of every one of my experiences inevitable?* And while that seemed impossible, most people assumed traveling through time was impossible as well. I really wished I could have that conversation with Dr. Nelson and Ms. Bergman. The impulse to dial in that meeting was intense, but I resisted.

The second conflict in my mind was the philosophical question that had haunted me from the beginning of my adventure. *Was it right? Was it wrong? Was it even feasible to change history to make something right? And, for that matter, was it ethically right to change something back to its original history after having changed that history?*

That multi-tiered conundrum left me despondent. And staring at my reflection in the mirror with my own recriminations and no resolution, I felt acutely alone. I had the distinct notion that there would be no answers to those questions until my Judgment Day.

The third conflict was easy to identify, and easy to resolve, but in light of the prior two issues, I knew I could not do it. Every fiber in my being wanted to jump to Beaumont and meet Tanya, immediately. I knew I had practically indefinite vacation time saved up, because I did not have a real life. All I really had to do was call work and tell them I was going to take a couple of weeks off. I caught myself at least a dozen times signing into my phone just to look at Tanya's address on my EXL Jump app. I desperately wished I had taken a selfie with her, some place where we were both alive and not covered in blood. To say that I missed her was a gross understatement. Looking in the mirror, I vowed I would never speak her name to anyone. That did not help my despondence.

Attempting to shift my focus, I pondered what I had learned through my time travel experience. There was a lot. And I knew there would be more as things processed.

The greatest lesson was sadly attached to the greatest loss I had experienced. I had been pursuing the wrong priorities my entire life. The deepest satisfaction I had experienced was being held by the one that I loved, late in life. In painful regret, I knew that I would never actually have that experience in real life.

Flashing back, I had the haunting remembrance of Ellen. My selfish actions had deprived her of a lifetime of every experience. That guilt burned bright in my mind every time I considered anything pleasurable. I resolved that there was never going to be reconciliation in that part of my memory.

I had readied myself to go to work without any conscious thought. I assumed that was a good thing. My mind was obviously occupied otherwise. And as I headed out the door, I had the acute anxiety that I might have dreamed the whole thing, and thinking about it so much was proof that I had lost my sanity. The paper sack with the bloody clothing was a grim reminder that reality and insanity might not actually be detached from each other.

I threw the bag into my BBQ grill and soaked the whole thing down with lighter fluid. Stepping back, I tossed a lit match into it. As I watched the only tangible reminder of my escapade disintegrate into ashes, I wondered if Farren was disposing of his evidence in the same way. I could almost hear his mother questioning his actions.

My mind flitted back to the scene in the hallway with Tanya and Eyelash Marsha. When I disappeared, it could have been a hysterically funny moment. Except the tremendous sense of loss would have kept Tanya from enjoying the event. Then it simply unhappened. My own sense of humor was blunted by my heartache.

I thought about my mother and her broken wrist, and I knew the real event had been decades prior. I pondered the irony that could have been, had I used the medical device invented by her grandson to heal her, two generations before he was born. I tried to sort out if that would have even been possible. And if it was possible, I wondered if it could have actually changed history that already existed.

My head hurt going around that giant theoretical merry-go-round. I suddenly wanted to drop in and see Tanya somewhere, but once again managed to stop myself.

I determined that we were going to destroy the phones and the programs on the very day, and just a few hours before, we made our initial simultaneous time jumps. That thought was the only thing that kept me from losing my mind. *Or*, I wondered, *does it prove I've lost it?*

I walked into the office without any recollection of the commute. And I was halfway surprised to find the place not crawling with police. I was relieved, but mysteriously disappointed in the ordinariness of the office. I had a paranoid sense that everyone was watching me, and I discreetly checked out my clothes to make sure I was appropriately dressed. Everything looked right, and I strode past the receptionist's desk with the regular morning greeting, and walked into my office.

Like a Super Hero

Farren scared me half out of my wits when he jumped up from my chair. He looked as excited as a black Lab in a flock of pigeons. I do not know why I was surprised to see him back to his regular age, since the same effect had happened to me.

"I've been thinking about the age correlation and the frequency signatures and Dr. Nelson's serum. So I've been studying the electro-oscilloscope readings from our data files," Farren excitedly chattered as he held up printouts of our research. "And if you look right here, you can clearly see an algorithmic progression that is directly related to chronological time. All we would have to do is intercept that signal with a counter-harmonic so that it would flatline, thus convincing the cells that they were not changing."

He started to say more, but I interrupted him. "Are you out of your ever-lovin' mind? You died. I died. Tanya died. And I'm pretty sure Bergman died. A war was ignited, and I had shoot-to-kill orders on me in multiple time zones. And you're treating this like it's a sport!"

As if he had not heard a word I said, he picked up his explanation with, "The only trick is, I have to figure out how to keep the cells believing that sense of timelessness without maintaining a steady supply of power through the phones. I bet Dr. Nelson could have given us an answer for that problem immediately."

"You didn't hear a word I said," I insisted.

"But I'm thinking that a secondary impulse that blocks that cell signal, sort of an electronic doorjam, could be possible," he chattered on excitedly.

"I'm talking to a wall," I complained.

He never broke stride. "There's also this trace signal that seems to be linked to both the chrono-signal, my term, and this sine wave that feeds back into the chrono-signal. There is a clear mathematical rhythm between the two lines. My theory is that they can be tied into an infinite loop and hold the age even after the power source from the phone is stopped. And by infinite, I mean a programmed amount of time."

"No!" I demanded. "We've got to burn the software and destroy the hardware!"

"Really? You think that stops the inevitable? How did Dr. Thaddeus get it then?" Farren challenged.

"Dr. Thaddeus? ... Dr. Khatri and Thaddeus used my notes from my senior year science fair project, which I stored in my dad's safe ..." I stopped mid-sentence. "I've got to find that safe and get those notes and destroy them."

"Do you have any idea where that safe is now?" Farren asked.

I looked down at my phone and knew the answer. I had not seen the safe since I went off to college. "It's probably still in the house my family used to own," I replied weakly.

"Well," Farren said happily, "You could break into the house, break into the safe, and maybe not get shot in the process. And if you're a really good cat burglar, you might not even go to jail. Too bad you don't have a magic ring like Bilbo. Or," he paused for an overly-dramatic time, "with a few taps on your phone, you could walk into your dad's study, ask him to open the safe, take **your** drawings out, and dispose of them at your convenience. History saved in one easy time jump."

I did not have a good argument for him. I knew I needed to destroy those old drawings. "No improvements to the time jump technology. I'm going back, getting the drawings, and then we are going to put this insanity to an end." I realized I was emphatically poking my finger at him as I spoke.

Farren nodded and whispered, "That would be a great time to introduce Tanya to your parents."

I threw my stapler at him. "That's a pretty raw subject in my mind at the moment," I snapped.

"Wow. Workplace violence. Maybe I need security," he mocked.

"What you need is to realize just how dangerous even the simplest time jump can be. It's just too risky," I reasoned.

"You went to an awful lot of effort to save Tanya," he reminded me. "I wasn't even there and I can tell it was harrowing. Now you're letting it all go?"

I looked at him with dead sincerity and explained, "You can't understand the sense of loss, and guilt, I would have dealt with if I had left her dead in my wake. Her life meant ... means, more to me than my own."

Farren's expression instantly clouded and I thought he was going to cry as he replied quietly, "I know exactly how it feels."

"What?" I snapped. I guess I had always known he had a sweet spot for Ellen but, for whatever reason, he had never actually worked up the nerve to ask her out.

That subliminal knowledge was undoubtedly the major contributing factor to the guilt burden I had assumed when her life had been cut short. In my attempt to suppress my overwhelming sense of guilt, I had poured my energy into the mission to undo my role in her death. But I had never actually considered what her story might look like if she had a full life span. I also had not given any thought to what a difference it may have made in the lives of others, including Farren. My self-centered perspective of the entire event turned inside out with that moment of revelation.

Subdued, I asked, "Why didn't you ever ask her out, or at least let her know you were interested?"

He shrugged.

"You could have jumped into the past and asked her to the prom before the blind date debacle," I suggested.

"Why didn't you do that instead of jumping into the crazy future?"

He shrugged again and admitted, "I don't know. I was afraid, maybe."

"Of what?" I asked, baffled. "That doesn't seem very logical for a guy who thinks in algorithms."

His shoulders slumped despondently, and I had the sudden realization that he was entirely insecure about how to approach a relationship. Not that I was an expert. And a life of hoping for the chance at the impossible was safe. But when the reality of time jumping was before us, he had not known what to do with it. "Tanya could have helped with that." I answered the question from our unspoken conversation.

We sat in silence for a few minutes listening to the wall clock tick. "Ten minutes and we need to get to work," I commented. "I don't know what's the right thing to do regarding Ellen. I think the first order of business is to recover and destroy those old drawings that I put in the science fair. Dr. Khatri was working with organized mobsters to make the time machine and … that can only make things worse."

Farren nodded in silence.

"Can I pull that off in ten chronological minutes?" I mused rhetorically. "I was just starting to get comfortable not being on any official shoot-to-kill list anywhere."

"Are you going to destroy your entire presentation and skip the science fair?" he asked surprised.

"No. That changes a lot of history. I need to take the notes from Dad's safe when no one is around, some time between when I put them in and whenever he got rid of the safe. If no one sees me, or at least no one sees me do something out of the ordinary, I think we're good." My theory seemed simple enough, but we both knew that was a busy time, as it all happened in the same week that Ellen died.

"I'm coming with you," he announced.

"No. I've got to drop into my room and get into appropriate clothing. Then I can move around my house as if I'm me." My response made sense in context. "You hold down the fort here. Okay?"

He gave me a thumbs up and I selected late afternoon, the day after I had put the packet into the safe, then pressed the button. I landed in my room and studied the place for a few minutes to get in touch with my inner eighteen-year-old.

I knew my performance would have to be really good if I was going to seem normal to my parents. Marveling at the horrible styles of my clothing, I got dressed. *They don't make 'em like they used to,* I thought. *It's a miracle I let myself out in public like this.*

I strolled through the house and into the den without anyone mentioning that my heart sounded like a bass drum. I walked past my dad, who was engrossed in the newspaper, and went to the empty spot where the safe had been sitting for as long as I could remember. My heart must have gotten really quiet, because I was sure it stopped.

When I could breathe again, I asked, "Hey, Dad? Where's the safe?"

Without looking up he replied, "Dr. Marsh, the dentist your mom doesn't like, bought it."

I tried to be casual. "Um, I had a packet in there with some of my science fair stuff. Is there a way I can get that from him?"

"It was empty. I checked before they picked it up," was his reply.

"I hid it under the piece of carpet in the bottom. Did you check there?" I asked hesitantly.

The newspaper came down and he looked at me across the top of his glasses. "Why ever would you hide something there?" Then without waiting for a reply, he added, "You'll have to call the dentist if it's that important. But I suppose it's still at the locksmith's getting the combination changed."

I almost asked for the dentist's number, but remembered we had phone books for such inquiries. *How many locksmiths do we have in town?* I wondered. I picked up a phone book as I casually wandered back to my room. With my door closed, I hurriedly flipped through the pages. *How does a town this size support six locksmiths?* I thought in exasperation.

I considered my options and did not like any of them. I could not remember the precise time I had put the packet into the safe. It had been unlocked for all of the years I could recollect. But if I walked back into the den and took the packet out, five minutes after putting it in the safe … that could be hard to explain. If I walked in and looked for it before the time I had put it in the safe, I had a different problem, because I could not remember where I had kept it. I hit the back button and landed in my office thirty seconds after I left.

Farren jumped. Then, glancing at the prize I had in my hand, blurted, "That's a phone book, not a science fair packet. What's going on?"

I hastily filled him in on the events at my house, and he nodded appreciably. "Your clothes are hideous, by the way," he remarked.

"Yeah, you were my fashion mentor. So, maybe don't laugh too loud," I retorted.

"Blind leading the blind," he replied with a sad shake of his head.

"We're wasting time," I reminded him.

"You either have to break into the locksmith shops until you find the right one, or you can wait till they open tomorrow morning, in that time zone. Or you have to keep trying to get the right timing at your house until the safe is still there and no one else is around." Farren basically reiterated the options I had considered. "Did you think to check on the fridge to see if there was a note about the time for the locksmith to pick up the safe? It would have taken a professional moving team to get that pig out of the house without breaking everything."

"Oh! Man! I forgot about the dry erase board!" I exclaimed. I somehow remembered to grab the phone book, then I jumped back to my old room.

Meandering into the kitchen was apparently not outside of the habitual practices of my youth. I opened the refrigerator, but my mind was so occupied with the anticipation of my mission that I could not think of what to snack on. So I grabbed a carrot, and took a bite with all the casualness my panic-stricken mind would afford. As the door closed, I looked at the board, and just then my mom called out from the living room, "Honey, are you eating a carrot?" The wonder in her voice told me that I was acting way out of character.

In my distracted state I replied, "They say between eight and nine, you shouldn't ..." I realized I had mixed my lame story with the time I was reading on the board. "You know, the last hour or two before bed, you shouldn't eat junk food."

My stilted response must have satisfied her curiosity, because she just mused to herself, "My baby is growing up."

I practically ran to my room and made the jump back to 6:30 in the morning that same day. It was perfect. I slipped into the den unnoticed and, miraculously, the safe was there and unlocked as it had always been. I grabbed the manila envelope from under the rug and almost laughed out loud. As I walked back to my room, my mom said, "You're up early."

"Busy day planned," was all I replied as I closed the door on the conversation.

I quickly changed clothes and, grabbing the precious envelope, I said, "Sayonara, Dr. Khatri! You and your Sicilian mafia!" Then I pressed the button.

The euphoria I felt when I slapped that envelope onto the desk in front of my friend was nothing short of intoxicating. I looked at the wall clock and declared, "I just saved the world in under three minutes! That right there is how it's done!"

We high-fived and I plopped down into my chair and suddenly felt exhausted.

Farren asked, "Is that technically changing history, since it hasn't happened yet?"

It seemed like he was leading to something. I retorted, "If you're trying to manipulate me into a hostile concession about being time lords, it's not going to work."

"I'm serious," he replied. "All you've done is changed your activity based on a better view of long term consequences."

Glaring, I grunted noncommittally.

"Besides that," Farren pointed at my office safe as he spoke. "The drawings aren't destroyed yet. This may be the safe your buddy in the future buys."

Without a word I slid my shredder out from under my desk. I gave Farren the kind of look a pitcher gives the batter just before he knowingly throws the final strike to win the World Series. I dumped the contents from the envelope onto my desk and was instantly numb with shock.

There were only random newspaper clippings.

"Where are the drawings?" Farren blurted in disbelief.

Newspaper clippings scattered across the desk and onto the floor as as I frantically sifted through the pile.

Flipping the envelope over, I read the label that I had written so many years prior. "Time Travel Machine Plans, by Chadwick Thompson. Top Secret."

Grand Theft Future

"Did you hide them somewhere else ... and label this packet as a decoy? Did you already destroy the drawings back then and forget? Who else had access to the safe?" Farren's questions came rapidly.

"Anyone had access to the safe! It was never locked. But I don't think anyone was around. My parents wouldn't have cared if they found the packet. I showed them my entire presentation and they just smiled and nodded. They didn't believe it was possible, but thought the theory was interesting ..." I cut off the inventory of the past abruptly when my phone lit up. "Why is my phone updating?" I turned and flashed a suspicious glare at Farren.

He held up two fingers up. "W-h-a-t? Two lines of code. That's all. It was really that simple."

I must have looked exasperated, because he further explained his update as if it justified his actions. His excitement was evident. "A little star will appear in the top right hand corner of the screen. Press that when you jump and you will be ageless."

"We're supposed to be cleaning up this mess." I whispered to keep my agitation within the walls of my office. "Not making it easier to stir up more problems! What is wrong with you? We need to be done with time jumping!"

Farren pointed to my empty packet and asked bluntly, "Where are the drawings? Can you find them from this office?"

I knew he was right. There was no possible way we could unravel the location of the missing drawings without doing at least one more time jump. As I mused about the inevitable, I was struck with a sudden impulse. "Dr. Khatri has jumped time and taken the drawings, because he knew I would jump back and destroy them."

Shaking his head, Farren dissented, "He couldn't fuel that much of a jump."

"Maybe he developed a better power source and jumped from a few years after we left him," I countered.

"You left him. I might have left him in limbo," Farren remarked.

"I didn't know he was working with organized mobsters," I retorted in my own defense.

Picking up a newspaper clipping, Farren said, "Science Fair 1996. Looks like this was from the day of the science fair."

We looked at each other and expressed the same thought simultaneously: "One of the judges."

My anger was strangely fueled by the sense of personal vindication that at least one of the judges had realized my wild invention had promise. I looked up at Farren who had glanced at the clock. "Time for work," he said.

"No more modifications to the time machines," I admonished while pointing accusingly at him.

As Farren left my office, I could tell he was not going to be productive that day. The truth was, I was not able to keep my mind on work either. I mentally replayed a thousand memories and, every time I tried to refocus on the present, one condemning theme kept echoing in my mind. I realized that I had been very detached from the personal lives of my coworkers, and I felt an urgency to repair that failure. When my secretary, Judy, walked in with the first report of the day, I greeted her as normal, then asked, "How are the kids doing these days?"

She seemed startled and hesitantly replied, "Terrence is testing for his brown belt this weekend. And Ramona wants to quit ballet and take up Taekwondo like her brother."

I did a quick memory search of their family dynamics and remembered the girl had some kind of heart surgery as an infant. I asked, "Is that okay with the doctor? I mean, with her heart thing."

Judy looked at me funny and replied, "That's been done a long time now. She's good. We just have so much invested in her dance training."

I felt stupid knowing I had probably been told all of those things before.

"You've got a lot on your mind, don't you?" she asked.

I nodded. "Yeah. I suppose I do."

"I have a little sign on my desk that says, 'The Fate of the World Is Not on Your Shoulders.' I look at that every time it feels like things are crashing in."

Her words were intended to be an encouragement. I smiled weakly and thanked her for the uplifting thought. But inside, my mind was frantically trying to make sense of my plight. *The truth is,* I had the mortifying thought, *the fate of the world is quite literally on my shoulders.*

Judging by the torrent of updates that my phone made, I assumed Farren was having trouble focusing on work as well. We met in the cafeteria at lunchtime and I hissed, "Why are you doing so many updates to the program we're about to destroy?"

"Making your life better is what I do," he casually replied.

"I don't think you remember the gravity of your situation when you were dead for so long!" I snapped back irritably. Someone in line turned around to look us over, and I abruptly terminated my rebuke.

"Mutual tracking, mayday call for aid, jump to assist, and voice response command recognition, are but a few of the new features at our fingertips. Actually, the voice response is at your vocal intonation-tips. And, you will need to enter that biometric data before it can be activated on your phone." Farren's laundry list of new features sounded like a marketing program.

"Um, are you planning on going to work today?" I asked irritably. We had been ignoring the people around us, and I took a quick glance around. No one seemed to show any interest in our conversation since I had quit talking about Farren's death. I suspected they just dismissed us as members of the mad-scientist club.

Farren never broke stride, but asked, "Where's Chad?"

My phone vibrated and his phone spoke back with a latitude, longitude, date, and time. He looked triumphant and responded, "I'm working on the lat-long interface with standard location descriptions. And I put in for a vacation day today."

"How about tomorrow?" I challenged.

He smirked, "Tomorrow's Saturday. And this Saturday is National Time Travel with Your Local Physicist Day. We've got to find those drawings to keep them out of the wrong hands, you know."

I looked at my lunch and mused, "I'm not entirely sure we are less of a global threat than the Sicilian mobsters."

"Oh, come on. You're overly dramatizing things," he challenged. "Every major technological advancement in history has had a rocky beginning. You've probably worked out the worst of the bugs already."

"You've heard my mom's monologue about when she broke her wrist on the ladder to my dad's treehouse." I waited for him to nod affirmatively around the over-sized bite he took from his deli sandwich. "I guarantee you that story has changed. In fact, I'm willing to bet that if you called her right now and mentioned it, she would tell you that the treehouse was haunted. That they'd heard whispers just before she fell."

Farren pointed at my plate and casually mentioned, "Your meatloaf is getting cold."

Sometimes you just have to cut your losses, and I did so right then. I knew we would have to revisit that argument after we had recovered my missing drawings. But until that time, I did not have much collateral to negotiate with.

"It's twenty-seven after noon," Farren said. "Do you know what that means?"

I was about to make a snarky reply, but he beat me to the punch. "We are twenty-seven minutes into the future. All that history has been permanently unmade. Not one thing we did by time jumping was left done. Don't you see? We have the ability to erase our mistakes as we go." His description of our experience was far too glib for my mood. Triumphantly he added, "Just put that into your paradigm cooker."

"We assume," I emphasized the words, "that everything we caused was undone. What if the war is still raging in 2276? What if Tanya is still crying in 2048? What if I'm still wanted in all those time zones, and I wake up one day with shoot-to-kill orders against me when we get there in time?"

I was warming up. I hissed, "And let's not forget that we have permanent scars from injuries incurred. And I, at least, have had an indescribable emotional trauma. And, I shouldn't forget to mention, that we are three days older than our current age!" I paused for a minute, then snapped, "Don't omit those details from your happy little world."

Farren shrugged. "I think you've overrated those possible troubles," was all he replied.

Set a Thief ...

That night I spent most of my time researching the
contest and judges of the science fair that my drawings
had been stolen from. I created a spreadsheet, of sorts,
with any pertinent-seeming information about each of
the suspected judges. I really wanted to end up with a
logic problem that was a simple process of elimination.
Unfortunately, there was nowhere near enough
information to make up a logic grid. In all of the data I
could retrieve from online sources, there was nothing
that set any of my suspects apart as more likely or less
likely to be the thief. The only exception was Mrs.
Hartman, who was a science teacher from my high
school. Since she had died about two years after the fair,
I wrote her out of the script. That left six suspects. I got
discouraged.

Somewhere in that research, I gave in to the
temptation to look up Tanya on Facebook. Her security
was set tight. But, thanks to a mutual friend from
college who had commented on some of her posts, I was
able to see a few posts. I studied Tanya's post about the
protracted hurricane power outage. It had been posted
earlier that day, and I searched for any hint that she
might remember me. There was nothing. I debated long
about commenting, but ultimately decided against it.

As I shaved that evening, I contemplated my life and
experienced a new low. *It's Friday night. I'm a bachelor.
And I have no reason, nor desire, to go out and do
anything social. All I want to do is find the missing
drawings and dispose of them properly.* **This** *is what a
life loser looks like.*

Saturday morning, I woke up early to my phone vibrating. I looked and there was an indicator that showed I had been "pinged." Before I could make a reply, Farren texted, "Just making sure you didn't do anything rash during the night."

I texted back, "Maybe I did and just got back home."

His reply was almost instantaneous, and I realized I had been played. "Haha! The tracker feature shows a full history."

For the first time since he had told me about the upgrades, I perused the new features. I had to admit that they were impressive. But I was not about to admit that to Farren. I texted back. "Stalker! I'm making my next time machine from a refrigerator box!"

I quickly checked Tanya's Facebook status, but there were no updates that I could see. I knew I was looking for an excuse to contact her. I also knew that was out of the question. I texted Farren, "I've compiled data on all of the judges from the science fair. We need to make it make sense."

He texted back, "There's an algorithm for that."

My reply was, "I figured that would be your response. Stop by after breakfast. Maybe we can save the world by lunchtime."

When we put all the bits of information on the table, it looked grim to me. Farren had insisted that for true mathematics to work, all the factors needed to be in the equation, so Mrs. Hartman was included with the other suspects. I recited the lineup, "Hartman, Gibbs, Johnston, Moore, Meeks, McCain, Gomez. They were all high school science teachers. I don't think I realized that back then. None of them have any substantial money. No extravagant vacations. No exciting scandals. Their families all seem to be intact, plus or minus a few divorces. Hartman and Moore are deceased. Gibbs was the chairman of the school district's science fair program. He took a job as principal of a charter school in D.C. nine years ago. Seems to be in the news every so often with accolades for his students' performances.

Gomez and Meeks are retired. Meeks took a trip to Vegas, but social media posts basically are of him and his wife eating at all the buffets. Not sure why they bothered to go to Vegas. McCain and Johnston are still at the same schools as they were back then. Johnston took a cruise to Alaska in 2009. Not much on Ms. McCain. No social media. Seems like the most capable of secrecy, since she's basically hidden from the public. But she pops up in church pictures frequently. Maybe that's a smokescreen." I paused my monologue for Farren to comment, but he was busy working out a formula on his tablet. "How do you make any sense of that?" I finished rhetorically.

After a prolonged silence where he poked away at his screen, Farren declared, "Suspect prioritization puts Gibbs at the top of the list with whopping 41% probability! Algorithms favor physical proximity to the scene of the crime at 100%. The number two suspect is Meeks. It appears that going to Vegas is a byproduct of committing crimes. Sort of a mathematical guilt by association."

"That hardly seems legit," I remarked.

Farren defended his results. "It's pure science. Pure statics. But, it doesn't matter. I think we've located our thief in D.C. You can lie with statistics, but the statistics themselves never lie."

I asked, "Can it really be that simple?"

Farren nodded. "Better living through mathematics," he replied.

"Now what? We break into his house, find the safe, and ... magically become safe crackers?" I asked with my sincerity and sarcasm running about fifty-fifty.

He pondered a moment, then asked, "Do you think we can jump into his house and jump back with the safe?"

Shaking my head, I replied, "I don't know about a non-living mass that size. Dr. Khatri's time machine took a lot of power to transport. I'm guessing that was mass related. Beside that, we'd be in possession of stolen merchandise."

"Nah," he replied. "We jump to tomorrow and bring it back today. That gives us plenty of time to get a locksmith to get in, get your plans, and jump back out."

"A-n-d, we have a locksmith on retainer that will keep a secret … indefinitely?" I queried skeptically.

"We'll find someone," Farren retorted irritably.

"Listen. I've spent all of the time I ever intend to in jail. This is getting dangerously close to criminal," I insisted. "And it proves my point. We've got to shut down the time travel thing ASAP!"

"Maybe," Farren held up both hands as if he was physically stopping me. It was his way of emoting excitement. "Maybe, **we** are meant to be the monitors. The time wardens. Time lords, if you will. Maybe this is the point in history where it all begins. And we're trying to throw away the tools that can make that happen?"

"No," I corrected irritably. "**I'm** trying to throw away the tools that can make that happen," My voice was increasing in pitch and volume, but I could not stop it. "**You're** trying to live in a made-up, delusional reality that doesn't exist!"

My phone buzzed and we both stared at it for a long moment. Confused, I looked at Farren suspiciously and asked, "Why are you buzzing me? I'm right here."

He looked at his phone. "I got that one too," he muttered absently as he scrolled through his apps.

"Well?" I asked impatiently.

"Huh, I didn't really think that one would work," he replied without looking up from his screen. "It appears that my experimental dragnet app might actually work."

"Does it change the names to protect the innocent?" I asked using my best Sergeant Joe Friday accent.

Ignoring my humor, he muttered to himself, "It looks like there may have been a time jump from 2255 to 2259." He looked up for the first time and added, "It's all in code. I didn't know it would work, so I didn't bother making an interpretive display."

I was stupefied. When I could finally form words, I asked, "Does that mean what I think it means?"

"Dr. Khatri," he replied. "Has to be. It can't be good."

"Or the Sicilians," I added with as much faux cheerfulness as I could muster. "Because that would be **so** much better." I was sure he was ignoring me. "Maybe they'll pay us a visit next."

The phones buzzed again. I said, "Please tell me that's a reminder and not a new jump."

"Fifty-nine to sixty," he interpreted aloud. "They're looking for something specific."

"We're running out of time," I said so casually I surprised myself. "They're looking for a weapon, or possibly a better power source. The one I designed back then would not be sufficient to jump back this far."

"They're coming to kill us?" Farren asked tremulously.

I nodded. "It's inevitable."

"Your buddy, Thaddeus?" he added.

Contemplating the big man's actions from when we had been in the hospital, I replied, "I don't think he had that in him. I think he was caught up in something that he couldn't escape. My guess is, the mobsters repossessed the time machine as payment for the loan."

Farren nodded soberly and the phones buzzed again. "You're kidding me!" My nerves were jangled.

"Later in sixty," he said flatly.

"We have to get that safe," I reiterated with urgency.

... To Catch a Thief

As Farren researched Mr. Gibbs' address and the filed floor plan of his house, I looked up his work schedule. When we had the information necessary, I had an idea. "How about we meet him on the sidewalk and I confront him about the packet of drawings. Maybe he will return it without us actually having to break any laws."

"What if it doesn't work?" Farren challenged. "Then he's aware that we are after the drawings."

"We jump back sixty seconds and pass him on the sidewalk like nothing happened. It will unhappen. Then we go to Plan B," I replied.

Grudgingly, Farren agreed. We jumped to Monday morning and amazingly came around the corner as Mr. Gibbs was walking to his car. I was surprised by his age.

"Good morning, Mr. Gibbs," I called out. "I've come to collect my time machine drawings from you. I know they're in your safe. And I won't press charges if you hand them over promptly."

His motions were shuffling and much more deliberate than I had expected, even for his age. He looked up and down the street slowly as he stood about to enter the car. Then he looked back and, in a shaking voice, replied, "I think you may have me confused with someone else, son. Who is it you are looking for?"

"Are you Mr. Gibbs, the science teacher?" I asked. I had the sudden notion that we were talking to the wrong man. I felt my phone buzz and was momentarily distracted.

"Yes, yes. Are you one of my former students?" His shaking voice still sounded confused.

"No. I was a contestant in the science fair in '96," I
replied. "I came to retrieve my entry drawings."

He looked even more puzzled. "I don't recall anyone
ever leaving their projects behind," he muttered. "If
they were, they would have been held by the hosting
school and cleaned out at the end of the school year."

"Sir. Someone stole my plans. I just want them back." I
tried to sound forceful, but knew that had been lame.

"Sadly, those kinds of shenanigans happen from time to
time," he replied. "I hope you reported that to the
department head at the hosting school. What year did
you say that was?"

"Um, '96," I answered and the look on his face became
more puzzled.

He remarked, "Seems like a long time to be worried
about such a petty thing."

My phone buzzed again and I threw caution to the
wind. Urgently I demanded, "Mr. Gibbs. You took my
drawings from the packet that I submitted, and you
replaced them with random newspaper clippings. My
time machine drawings are in your safe. And I want
them back immediately."

His puzzled look became even more confused. "I stole
your ...? What? Whatever your game is, the police are on
the way."

I figured Mr. Gibbs had hit an emergency call button
on his phone. I had expected as much. My phone buzzed
again and I jumped. Even Farren became agitated. Just
then we all heard the sound of a police siren coming our
way. Throwing his hands into the air in exasperation,
Farren blurted, "Khatri, or his cronies are really moving
around! They're not finding it, but their jumps are
getting closer. They're getting closer!"

"We should jump," I said as the police car skidded to a
stop behind Mr. Gibbs' car.

The officer jumped out and came running up, but
before I could hit the jump button, Farren shouted,
"He's stolen our blueprints and refuses to hand them
over!"

I looked up to see Farren striding forward and pointing at Mr. Gibbs as he made his accusation. I thought, *He really takes that statistical data as fact.*

The officer looked confused. "Who called 911?" he demanded.

"Our drawings are in his safe! And he won't admit it," Farren persisted hotly.

"Stand down, sir!" the officer commanded. Then looking to Mr. Gibbs, he asked, "Are these men threatening you?"

"They're trying to get me to open my safe," Gibbs replied in his quavering voice, "I think they want to rob me."

As the officer turned to confront us, he was reaching for his handcuffs, and I knew Plan A had failed. "Jump," I whispered as I touched Farren's shoulder.

We landed at the exact same spot as we had the first time. It was a half minute prior to our original landing, which allowed us to collect our senses. Mr. Gibbs tenuously ambled down his steps and we greeted each other amicably as we walked by his house. Once we rounded the corner, Farren exclaimed under his breath, "That was the coolest thing ever! We just undid a moment of history!"

I gave him a sidelong scowl. "Not history. It hasn't happened yet. We're two days into the future. Put that into your algorithm and gnaw on it," I replied. My phone buzzed again and I just shook my head. "Let's jump in."

We jumped into the house and landed a half minute before we left the sidewalk. After a quick look around I found a small personal lockbox. I was ready to grab it and jump, but Farren stopped me. "That doesn't look like anything someone would buy at an auction in the future," he whispered.

I knew he was right, but I thought we should bring it along just in case. We found the real safe in a spare bedroom. It was not as large as my dad's safe had been, but too heavy for us to lift. "Will it travel with us?" Farren asked with obvious concern.

"Do we have a choice?" I asked.

We landed back in my house with a thud. I was simultaneously elated, astonished, and dismayed that the safe had made the jump with us. My phone was flashing red and I realized even that little jump had drained the battery. "Mass. Mass is as much a part of the equation as time and distance," I muttered more to myself than Farren.

"That would make sense," Farren replied.

As soon as I plugged in the charger, my phone buzzed again. "Where are they now?" I asked.

"February, 2261. They've been jumping around a small area in the same time for a while. They've obviously found what they want. But they must be having difficulty taking it." Farren's supposition seemed reasonable.

"Locksmith time," was all I replied.

By the time the locksmith arrived, I was practically a basket case. Having two stolen safes in my living room was enough stress, but the irregular timing of the dragnet apps buzzing kept me on constant edge.

To my consternation, the locksmith popped the little lockbox open with a small slotted screwdriver. That took about two seconds. I quickly rummaged through the various papers inside. They were all school-related contracts and school board notes.

The locksmith used a stethoscope on the old safe. He looked so much like a movie safe cracker, I wondered if he was faking. It took about five minutes, which felt like five weeks. When he turned the lever up and pulled the door open about an inch, I almost gasped.

I paid the man with cash and, as soon as he was down the steps, we looked into the safe. There was everything from his passport to an antique revolver engraved with the name Elmer Gibbs. I assumed from the age of the gun, Elmer must have been his grandfather. There was a box of jewelry, a medicine bottle with some gold flakes, and a half-dozen WWI medals. There was big folder full of insurance papers, which I looked through thoroughly.

And other than that, there were a few keepsakes that hardly seemed important enough to place in a safe.

There was no rug and, after carefully rapping on every surface to find any secret compartments, I was at a loss. "Nothing," I said with dismay. "Nothing. Now what?"

Farren was as perplexed as I was. "Man. I feel really guilty about haranguing that old man now," was all he replied.

"We've got to get this stuff back. And we need a Plan C quick," I stated the obvious.

It only took a few seconds to jump Mr. Gibbs' safe and lockbox back into his house. When we jumped back home, I felt a lot better about the stealing part. But we were no closer to finding the drawings.

"How about we go back and try to see the thief when he takes the drawings?" Farren suggested.

I had considered that earlier, but dismissed the idea, because students were not allowed into the staff room where the judging took place. However, I had forgotten that Farren had uploaded the non-aging feature. That changed everything. "How long will the anti-aging feature last when we jump out?" I asked.

Farren shook his head slowly. "I'm not sure. It's a signal interceptor that reprograms the wave and fires it into the cell signaling system. So, it can't possibly last more than seven days. I would think more like eight to twelve hours. Maybe slightly longer if you're dehydrated."

I contemplated the biological variances and remarked, "I'm guessing if you are too far dehydrated, it won't work at all. Maybe Dr. Nelson could give us a definitive answer."

"Nice try," Farren said. "You know where she lives. Why don't you just look her up and give her a call?"

"Yeah, don't do that," I retorted. "We're working to end the possibility of unethical uses of time travel. Not write a new how-to book on the subject."

Farren snorted back, "Hrump! There's nothing unethical about love."

"If there's a possibility of personal gain, there is no way to completely isolate selfishness from the paradigm," I countered.

"Okay, Reverend. As time wardens, we're hereby sworn to celibacy. Maybe we should call ourselves 'Time

Monks,' " Farren replied with a generous dose of sarcasm.

I rolled my eyes at his over-dramatization. "Let's jump to the sidelines of the judging. Should we jump ahead first, and age a little more? We could be senior staff members. Or are we incognito enough?" I asked.

"I think with our lab coats and work ID badges, we look authentic enough," he answered.

Our phones buzzed again and I began to feel desperate. "Your work ID is good. Mine will coincidentally match one of the candidate's names," I pointed out.

"It says 'Dr. Thompson' on it. How many kids have 'Dr.' in front of their name? Seriously. You're getting paranoid," Farren replied.

"Okay. Okay! I get it. Should we dress up better? I should comb my hair," I was nervously fidgeting about irrelevant details.

Farren shrugged and asked, "When was the last time you got called a mad scientist?"

"Yesterday. I get called that every day." I was not sure where his argument was going.

"Perfect! You're already dressed for the role." Grinning triumphantly, he added, "No one is going to give your badge a second look. Now, what time do we need to jump in?"

I recounted the events of that day. It was vividly etched into my memory. "The judging ended at noon. Everyone took a lunch break and reconvened at 1:00. Then the awards were announced. They started with the honorable mentions first. Pretty much, every entry that didn't win a place got an honorable mention. Next they did the third place, second, and first, in that order. You can imagine my excitement when my project wasn't in the honorable mentions. After second place, I was about to cheer. Then they called out some tire recycling project and I wondered if there was some confusion. Tire recycling had been going on for decades. Obviously, the judges did not have much imagination beyond political correctness. But, it never occurred to me that they were stealing the good ideas."

Farren nodded. "On the up side, they really did see the potential in your science. And, you have proved it. On the down side, you now think it was a horrible idea that needs to be destroyed before the world comes to an end."

"Let's go catch our thief," I retorted.

Our phones buzzed just as we were about to jump. Farren's last words in our organic time zone were, "They're headed this way."

We landed in the boiler room and silently peeked around the equipment to make sure no one was there. It was five minutes to noon, which gave us barely enough time to get to the classroom adjacent to the science room. I held my breath as we passed people I recognized. Enough years had passed for me that I could not remember most of their names. I had not given any thought to the possibility that someone might walk into the room we were in, until I was standing in the dark looking out through the half-closed door. Fortunately, no one came in.

At noon, the staff, teachers, and volunteers began to stream out of the science room for the lunch break. I had fully expected one of the judges to lag behind, so I was confused when I had seen all of them leave. But, Mrs. Hartman, my science teacher, stayed by the door until everyone else was out. At that point I was ready to nab her red-handed, but again, to my surprise, she locked the door and followed the crowd to the cafeteria.

Farren hissed, "Are you sure you actually entered your project in this science fair?"

In that moment, I began to doubt everything, including my own sanity. Our phones buzzed and Farren whispered, "They're tracking this way by twenty-year jumps. They're at 2141. Probably recharging their power cells. Either they didn't find the power supply they were looking for, or they were looking for something else, like a weapon."

"That's encouraging," I replied. "Possibly they were tracking down someone to rub out."

"Thaddeus?"

"If I was a betting man, I'd put money on it," I replied grimly. "Khatri is in. The mob wants their money. And Thaddeus was the only one among them with a conscience."

We heard the click of a door opening down the hall and held still. A few seconds later, the janitor passed our hiding place and went straight to the science room. He quickly unlocked the door and let himself in. I got a glimpse of his left hand and saw what could only be a stack of newspaper clippings. A minute later, he emerged with my drawings. I saw the heading on my project paper and was enraged. I suddenly wished I had a weapon, because the man was sturdy-looking. I remembered he was from Croatia. *Mr. Delich! Maybe he's a spy?* I thought, but dismissed the idea, since a high school would be a lousy place for a spy. Our phones buzzed again.

Ignoring my phone, I watched Mr. Delich head down the hallway. As expected, he turned into the boiler room. I rushed to the doorway with Farren on my heels. As we passed the boiler room, he closed the door to the boiler firebox. We turned the corner and did a quick about-face. I said to Farren, as if we were preoccupied with the contest, "I think the tire recycling has the most practical merit, as there are roughly eighteen million tires per year headed to landfills."

We nearly crashed into the janitor as he rounded the corner. He was talking excitedly into his cell phone, and I almost laughed about the antenna on his old phone. Fortunately I remembered we were back in 1996 before I said anything stupid.

We darted into the boiler room, and I examined the door to the firebox. The phones buzzed again and my blood pressure took a jump. I knew the boiler had been a duel fuel system. It was equipped with a natural gas burner, and the paper trash was burned in the coal box in the winter. Coal had not been used for years. The door was cold, which I expected. It was well into springtime and the weather was warm, so no fire would be necessary until the following winter.

I opened the firebox and there, on the coal grate, was a brand new manila envelope. I had a moment of panic that Mr. Delich was going to burn my drawings. I snatched up the envelope and quickly opened it. My examination revealed that the entire set of drawings was there. "They're all here," I whispered.

The phones buzzed again and Farren furtively checked their progress. "Twenty-five years out," he whispered urgently.

We heard footfalls in the hallway and slipped behind the boiler just in time. A student came in and opened the firebox. He was sweating profusely and his breaths were coming in ragged gasps. He pulled out a cell phone and began to make a call. As I peered from behind a maze of pipes and valves, I recognized him as a kid who had a severe drug addiction. I had always felt a little sorry for him, but at that moment, all I felt was a growing rage.

His side of the conversation went, "Hey, man. This ain't no joke, the package is gone. I need my stuff. You know. It's gone. I know what the boiler is, man. No! It's gone! I need my payment, man. I'm gonna get it from your car, man. I can't leave the envelope in the car. It's gone, man."

The phones buzzed again and the kid said, " Hang on, man. Someone's in here." He ended the call and looked around the corner.

I stepped out from behind the boiler and asked, "Are you looking for this?"

The boy looked startled. "Thief," he hissed.

"Nope. It's all got my name on it. I've come back from the future to take back my property which was stolen from me by the janitor. And in a few minutes, this room is going to be lit up with ray gun blasts from a bunch of mobsters that are traveling through time to try to beat us to these documents." I was intentionally telling the kid the straight truth. I did not have a plan, only I had some idea that maybe a little shock would scare him out of the boiler room.

Farren called out. "Chad ... They're at the library, in town, next week. Their next time jump is going to be here. They're going to kill us, if we don't get out of here."

I pointed at the boy and ordered, "Get to rehab today! Go! Get out now!"

Our phones buzzed, and the bewildered boy turned for the door. In one step, he collided with Dr. Khatri's time travel machine. The cumbersome box had suddenly materialized just like Farren had warned.

I threw the papers back into the firebox and frantically looked for the ignite button. My search was interrupted by Thaddeus. "Greetings, Dr. Thompson," he said wearily. And I knew something was seriously amiss. He continued, "If you would be so kind as to hand over those papers, we won't have to kill you."

A man that I fancied looked like a Sicilian mobster stepped out of the box behind Thaddeus. He had a rather boxy-looking weapon that had a very real looking barrel. I assumed it also shot very real bullets, based on what had happened in Dr. Khatri's shop.

"If you kill me, you'll have a major power grid shutdown in your time zone. I haven't invented that stuff yet." My rebuttal seemed to affect Thaddeus, but the gunman must have been too dull of wit to comprehend the ramifications of actions in different time zones.

Almost pleading, Thaddeus asked, "Please. They have my daughter, and they'll kill her if I don't bring back the drawings."

"So, Dr. Khatri sent you. He knew I would try to destroy the papers." I stated the question in my mind.

Thaddeus glanced over at the mobster and said, "They killed Dr. Khatri, once they figured out I was the one doing all the tech work. They won't stop, Chad. Just hand over the papers. Please!"

"Listen. Thaddeus. There's so much more to be had.
Why were you jumping around 2261 so much?" I looked
at the mobster and asked, "Hey, Guido. Why were you
guys jumping around in 2261 so much?"

He looked back and forth between me and Thaddeus
before he answered, "I'm Francisco. Guido is back
guarding the wife and kid."

"They were finding a place in history where I had a
wife and kid," Thaddeus answered almost in tears.
"They shot Khatri in front of us. My family and me. His
body is on the floor in my living room."

Farren called out from behind me, "Just give them the
time machine. They've found our secret lab. They've
caught us here with it. Let's just let them take it back
home with them. It's all we've got and so much better
than the papers that were lost."

Thaddeus shook his head ever so slightly and I knew he
was confused, but stalling. I asked, "Francisco, where
were you before you met Dr. Khatri? This time machine
will take you wherever you imagine. No settings or dials
to adjust." I was gesturing toward the boiler as I spoke.

Francisco motioned with his weapon and we all
stepped deeper into the boiler room for him to get by
the controls. "Turn on the infinity meter here." I pointed
to the gas valve. "And press the red button and hold for
a few seconds. Wherever you wish for, that's where you
will land," I explained. "Do you miss your family?"

He fell for it all the way. When he turned the gas valve,
a satisfying pressure hiss could be heard. The
permanently chiseled scowl on the mobster's face
softened into a genuine smile. He reached for the red
ignite button and, in that instant, Delich, burst through
the door. He was followed closely by the kid that had
tried to get the drawings to his car.

Cursing in Croatian, Delich gave the time machine a
contemptuous shove. It did not move and that seemed to
make the janitor more angry. Francisco pointed his gun
at Delich and did some cursing of his own in Italian.

Trying to cover everyone in the boiler room with his weapon, Francisco backed away from the boiler, and I saw Farren press the ignite button. Francisco saw the movement too, and swung his gun to bear on Farren. "Stop that!" he ordered frantically. And I saw his finger squeeze on the trigger.

"Look out!" I shouted and lunged for the janitor.

Francisco fired his gun as he spun to confront Delich. The bullet ricocheted off the side of the boiler and into the storage cabinet. As Delich and I tussled, it was obvious that he was stronger than I was. But, by the fury that comes with desperation, I managed to force him back against Dr. Khatri's time machine. In frustration, I hissed through gritted teeth, "Come on, furnace!"

I had Delich pinned, but he pulled his right arm free, so I head butted him in the chin with all I had. At that instant, the time machine, Thaddeus, and Francisco all vanished.

My force that had been pinning Delich against the time machine drove him hard into an aluminum stepladder that was hanging on the wall. His head connected with a sharp crack, and we all crashed to the floor. I jumped up, but Delich was out cold with a flow of blood coming from his lower lip. The kid, whom I suddenly remembered was named Jon, was crying in panic.

I looked over at Farren as he casually shut down the boiler. "Mission accomplished," he said with a grin.

We could hear frantic voices approaching, and I thought we would jump straight out, but Farren ran to the door and waived the approaching people to the boiler room. "The janitor has had a bad fall!" he cried. "Someone call 911!"

There were about a dozen people on the scene and, by good fortune, one of them was the school nurse. She grabbed a first aid kit and helped the groggily recovering janitor into a sitting position. "What day is it?" she asked him as we walked nonchalantly around the corner. I led Jon by the arm.

In his thick accent, I heard Delich say, "There was a spaceship in my room."

"Severe head trauma," the nurse said to someone who was on the phone with the emergency dispatch.

When we got around a corner, we stopped beside the door to an empty room, and I pointed my finger right up in Jon's face. "If you don't get into rehab today, they're going to lock you up in a nuthouse! There's no way to unsee what you've seen! But you can recover your life if you get help! That's all I know to tell you!"

I was sure the shock got through his chemical haze. I had no idea if it would do any good. I only knew we, as students, had basically looked the other way regarding his addiction. And that had not helped a thing.

"Goodbye, Jon. I wish you a happy and healthy life," I said as Farren and I stepped into the empty room. As soon as Jon could not see us, Farren pressed the jump-to-home button.

We landed in my living room, and the first thing he said was, "Our phones haven't buzzed since the furnace."

I felt such a flood of relief I could have cried if I was alone. "What took that thing so long to burn those papers?" I asked in a sudden backlash of emotion.

"The exhaust flue is at the back of the firebox, so it gets hottest there first. It takes a bit longer to get the front started," Farren explained.

He knew I was being rhetorical. "Thanks for that," I retorted sarcastically. "Too bad we didn't pick up that bullet. I hope the police don't find it."

"Oh, no ..." Then he gave me the stink-eye look that told me I had him for a second.

Summit to Plummet

The next week seemed like the most boring procession of time I had ever experienced. Farren was out of town all week, so it was Friday morning before we had a chance to debrief on the excitement of the prior weekend.

He walked into my office and unceremoniously dropped a book onto my desk. I looked down at it and wondered what it meant. "Unshackled from the Monster," I read the title aloud. "And ...?"

"I met this guy at the convention. He went to our high school, although he didn't remember you, or me," Farren replied.

"Okay. Well, I suppose it's nice to not be remembered badly," I replied tentatively.

"He said he lost his school years in a drug fog. Now he runs one of the biggest rehab ranches on the East Coast." Farren was watching me closely.

I grabbed up the book and saw the author, "Dr. Jon Rehnquist?" Looking up at Farren I asked, "Is that the same Jon? What does this mean?"

"We changed history for the better! Don't you see? There's merit to having the ability to correct things in the past." Farren was pleading like a lawyer.

I jumped up from my chair and frantically whispered, "No! We're not God! We shouldn't be messing with this thing! We don't even know for sure that this had anything to do with us!"

"One more jump," he begged. "One more and we can be done. All we need to do is stop Ellen from crossing those tracks."

That hit me hard, but I retorted hotly, "Then we launch into a whole new series of problems. Haven't you noticed how quiet our phones have been this week? No time-jumping hitmen hunting us down through history. Using our own library, for crying out loud! They looked at the newspaper, in our hometown library, to find the science fair times and dates! Does that not freak you out a little at least?" I was worked up.

"This was your intention all along, for all these years, to undo one wrong in your life. Now you have the ability to do so, and you refuse," Farren accused. "What's stopping you? What's stopping us from fixing this one thing?"

"What if it all goes wrong?" I asked. "What if turns out that she's not interested in you? Then what? What if we get killed in the process? What if it changes our lives dramatically?"

"It's Tanya, isn't it? You're afraid that the trajectory of your life might change too much. You're afraid you're never going to meet her, or ... you're going to forget her? Aren't you?" Farren's words hit close to home. "I don't think there is anything you or I or anyone can do to make you forget Tanya. I only knew her for a brief time, such as we count time, and it was obvious she was crazy about you."

We had a staredown in my office before I finally asked, "How do you propose we save Ellen from the train without derailing history any worse than that?"

Farren smiled and said, "I've given this a lot of thought. You don't have to do anything except get me the flares from the trunk of your mom's car. I'll go to that railroad crossing and, when I see the train coming and the car coming, I'll put out the flares on the road to warn her. I had tried to figure out how to fix the crossing lights, but since it was pouring rain, I was afraid I might get electrocuted."

I sat and pondered his plan for a long time. My only objection was that we were meddling with history ...

again. And I did not want to create any new problems. "Okay," was all I said.

"Awesome! Then after this, we can ditch the phones and time programs," he promised. I did not answer.

That Saturday morning we made our plan. We needed to get to our respective homes and wear age-appropriate clothing. I was slated to borrow my mom's car and drive to Farren's house, where we would transfer the flares to his car. Then I would go home and reverse my preparations and jump back out. From that point, Farren would be on his own. It seemed like it was a straightforward enough plan.

Nothing ever seems to go as planned. When I jumped into my old bedroom, the first thing I discovered was that my laundry was in the dryer in the basement. *Great*, I thought. *Now I'll have to sneak around in these clothes*. My phone buzzed, and I saw that Farren had made a jump back a few minutes. He jumped again and I knew he was having some difficulty. The jumping ended, but it gave me the idea to do a lateral time jump to the basement. I pressed the button, grabbed my clothes from the dryer, and jumped back to my room as the basement door was opening.

I got into my old clothes, and it occurred to me that I chose the same clothes that I had picked the last time I jumped in. I walked into the kitchen and asked, "Mom, can I borrow your car?"

"I've got to get it down to Sears for tires today. Use your dad's car," she replied.

Bummer, I thought. *I don't think Dad has flares in his car*. "Okay. Or I could drop it off for you," I called back to her.

"Thanks, honey, but I'm going to do some shopping while they do the tires," she answered and tossed me the keys to my dad's car.

I did not remember my youth car privileges being so liberal, but time has a way of skewing the memory. I went to the garage and was happy to find no one else there. I quickly transferred the flares into the trunk of my dad's car and, as carefully as I could, drove to Farren's house. I knew a traffic stop would be disastrous, as my wallet had ID from my organic time, and the cash money I had was not yet printed.

Somehow I made it to Farren's house without attracting any attention. It was raining when I opened the trunk to get the flares. He crawled out from under his car and, in exasperation, exclaimed, "I think the solenoid is bad! I've made a couple of jumps back in time to work on it longer, but I'm going to have to get to the parts store. Can you give me a ride?"

We were mostly quiet on the way to the parts store. I wondered if we were trying to cross a line that was off limits. *Is this God's way of stopping us from doing this?* I pondered to myself.

The lightning show was impressive as we trudged into the store. The parts man greeted us, and Farren put his starter on the counter. After going through the vital statistics, the man went into the back and reemerged a couple of minutes later with a box. The parts looked like they were the same, so Farren handed a card to the clerk. When he swiped the card in the reader, nothing happened.

I nudged Farren and suggested, "I think that one is not activated yet."

The clerk looked at the card for the first time and his eyes widened noticeably. "You've got a really long service date on this card," he said in wonder. But his demeanor abruptly turned to suspicion and he insisted, "I need to see some ID there, buddy."

Farren almost pulled his license out, but I caught his arm. "Time to take Farren home for his meds," I said. "We'll probably be back tomorrow with some of his daddy's cash."

I took the card from the startled clerk, handed Farren the old starter, then pushed him toward the door. I kept us moving until we were outside. He immediately demanded, "What was that all about? I can't give up now!"

"What was that all about?" I parroted. "How about, not
having an altercation with the police when we are, in
fact, holding cash that hasn't been printed, cards with
non-existent accounts, and ID that says we are in our
thirties," I hissed. "Does that sound anything like stolen
wallets to you?"

"Right. Right," he replied irritably as if he were coming
out of a trance. He looked at his watch and commented,
"We're running out of time again. I think we need to
jump back an hour."

I realized at that moment how deeply Ellen's death had
affected him. His decision making was based entirely on
emotion and not logic, and I really needed him to
consider the complexity of every jump we made. "Don't
forget that every time we do a back jump we
exponentially complicate the unwind. And everything we
don't properly unwind leaves a breadcrumb trail for
power hungry people, like Dr. Khatri, that will trace
back to us eventually. Don't kid yourself, if we figured
out how to time jump, someone else will too. If we
figured out how to track other time jumpers, someone
else will do that too. And the only way time jumping
gives someone power is if they have the exclusive ability.
Which means we're a target … technically, forever." I
paused to catch my breath and collect my wits before I
continued, "We're just going to jump back a couple of
minutes and redo this one event."

Farren nodded and I set us back two and a half
minutes. We landed beside my dad's car and made our
way through the rain into the parts store. The sense of
déjà vu never ceased to surprise me when I made those
short jumps back. The clerk's greeting was exactly as it
had been before and, when we were about halfway to
the counter, I stopped Farren and asked, "Did you
remember to get money from your dad?"

He played his role perfectly and, rolling his eyes, we
headed back for the door. Back then, Farren was always
working on his car and I wondered if the clerk

recognized him. "We'll be back when the weather gives us a break," I called out as a diversion.

"Good luck," the clerk replied, and in a few minutes we were at the light ready to pull out of the parking lot. By then, it was fully dark, and the weather made it seem darker as I turned on the right turn signal.

With the rhythmic ticking of the turn signal in my subconscious, I did a mental tally of the minutes, and it occurred to me that I was counting down to Ellen's death. It always seems odd, how the mind replays tragic events in slow motion. I had not been there, but the eyewitness account of the deadly encounter at the train crossing scrolled through my mind. Ellen had passed through the last intersection in town and headed straight for her family's farm. The witness, an elderly man who had a farm further out of town, pulled out behind her after the traffic light had changed. He was far enough behind that he could not tell what kind of car it was. The old man had reported that when Ellen's car approached the railroad crossing, the gate was up and no lights were flashing. He said that he had seen the train as it came into the curve, but Ellen apparently had not. It was too late when she slammed on the brakes. On the wet road, her car had hydroplaned sideways, and the collision took her life instantly. *Tunnel vision driving*, the authorities had labeled it. I knew the truth, that it was my fault that she was distracted. Involuntarily, I glanced at the clock on the dash. We had seven minutes.

"Light's green," Farren said absently.

I turned left onto the road, and he looked up sharply from his thoughts and asked, "Where are you going?"

Farren had been looking pale and seemed to be lost in a funk of thought. I wondered if he was sick from working in the rain for so many hours. But, I knew he had to be feeling the same sense of despondence as I had at our failure.

"If we rush it, maybe we can make it to the crossing before Ellen gets there," I replied with a little more optimism than I felt.

"Maybe we should just jump back and start over," he
offered.

The tone of his voice told me that he knew the same
painful truth that I knew. We had tangled a complicated
web in a narrow window of opportunity. To start over
risked setting other events into action that would almost
certainly have undesirable, and possibly far reaching,
consequences.

I pressed the accelerator. "You're going to get us killed
now," Farren gasped.

"Straight greens is our only chance to get through
town in time," I retorted determinedly.

"Going too fast doesn't make the lights turn green," he
snapped.

"I'm not going **that** fast," I shot back.

"Yellow," he called out and I knew we were not going
to make it.

I stopped for the red light and looked longingly at the
next three traffic signals. They were all green heading
straight out of town. I glanced at the clock. Three
minutes. I did a semi-panicked, mental calculation to
determine if Ellen had already been through the lights.
There were no other vehicles in sight.

When my light finally changed to green, I stepped on
the gas. At that moment, headlights came into view from
the left, at the next intersection.

Farren sat forward, straining to see through the
torrential rain, and gasped, "Ellen!"

The light turned yellow, and Farren ordered, "Get
ahead of her!"

I gunned the car, and entered the intersection on the
yellow light. Seemingly out of nowhere a shadowy figure
loomed in the crosswalk. A pedestrian, in dark-colored
clothes, was ambling across the road in the torrent. I
slammed the brakes and watched in detached horror as
my hands steered the car in a desperate attempt to
maintain control. We hydroplaned and miraculously
skidded around the pedestrian, who never looked up
from his shambling walk.

My car came to rest after barely hitting the curb and narrowly missing the mirror of a parked police car. I was shaking hard, but determined to stay ahead of Ellen. Then, before I had a chance to step on the gas again, the lights and siren of the police car came on. I pulled over two spaces in front of the squad car.

"Just go!" Farren urged, "We can jump back and fix this. Go!"

It was too late. The squad crept up behind me and Ellen drove by. Farren collapsed back into the seat in despair. "Oh my gosh," he blurted. And I knew he was on the verge of tears, because I was too.

It seemed to take a long time for the officer to get out of the squad car into the pouring rain. I knew it was going to be a bad encounter as I rolled down the window. "What's the problem there, son? I need your license, registration, and insurance card," the officer snapped. "And I'll need you to step out of the car."

I nervously fumbled for the registration and insurance cards. I produced them as I climbed out into the rain. I lied, "I forgot my wallet at home, officer. My name is Chadwick Thompson. This is my dad's car." Then, hoping to soften the encounter, I added, "I've had a particularly bad day, sir."

"Well, it's about to get a lot worse," he growled. "Get in the car." I was relieved that he pointed to the passenger side of the squad car and not the back seat.

Inside the car, he pulled up a clipboard with a violation report on it and asked, "Last name?"

I was not sure how I was going to deal with the ticket, but in my dismay I assumed Farren and I would jump back and undo the events anyway. I answered, "Thompson, with a P. T-H-O-M-P-S-O-N."

"First?" he asked. His tone was completely emotionless. It occurred to me that he had probably seen just about everything.

For a brief instant I considered doing a time jump to show him something new. I resisted the urge, but before I could respond to his question, a duel-tone alert came

across the radio. I started at the sound even as I looked
at the clock on his dash. My heart plummeted. Ellen had
just died.

The Dreaded Phone Call

"All units respond. Wreck at intersection of Potter's Creek Road and railroad crossing. Juvenile female in a white sedan. Crossing signal is not functioning. All units respond." The message came across the radio like an electrical jolt to my entire being.

I was in shock and only partially aware as the officer slapped my papers against my chest and ordered, "Get home, boy! And don't ever drive without your license again!"

I was not sure if I jumped out of his car, or if he actually pushed me out. But as soon as the door closed, he launched down the road at a speed that could not possibly have been safe. I realized I was crying and stood in the rain until I could regain control.

When I climbed into the car, Farren looked as white as a ghost. I nodded grimly, confirming what he already knew. With the best composure I could muster, I choked out, "It's worse hearing it in real time."

He nodded and turned away. We drove in silence, and two more police cars and an ambulance streaked past us heading to the railroad crossing. *They just as well slow down so no one else dies for this today*, I thought.

Once we got to Farren's house, we transferred the car parts into the trunk of his car, then went inside. Mrs. Helton saw us trudging in completely soaked and looking whipped. She immediately assumed we were at imminent risk of dying from pneumonia, and insisted we have large bowls full of hot soup. We managed to get the soup down without any incident, then we went straight to Farren's room. He had a basement lair that was the

perfect nerd man cave, which we had capitalized on
with our crazy schemes as teens. But that evening, as
soon as we were past where his mother could hear, we
began plotting our next move.

We plugged in our phones behind his desk, because
they were about two decades ahead of their time, and
we did not want his mom to see them. Then we began to
map our next jump.

"We should jump back to where you came to give me a
ride. Then go straight to the railroad crossing," Farren
proposed.

"I don't know. The number of obstacles that we faced
make me feel like we may be treading on God's toes," I
argued.

"Nobody treads on God's toes," Farren retorted. "Is it
possible to do wrong by trying to save someone's life?"

I pondered for a moment, then asked, "What if there is
a 'time limit' on this kind of thing? You know. In actual,
or organic time. Maybe that window has passed. It's
been twenty years."

"You should have just taken her to the dance," he
retorted. "It wouldn't have killed you. She's not even a
blood relative. Your mom's brother's wife's daughter, for
crying out loud."

The stinging insult of intentional peer derision never
seemed to dull. "It was a mockery. The whole 'fix the
nerd up with a blind date' was a set-up to make fun of
me, and her," I countered. "They planned all along to set
me up with my own cousin. And all of **them** assumed
she was a blood cousin, because we were, like, three
when Uncle Frank married Aunt Cheryl. And I don't
even remember that. I never think about her being a
'step' cousin. She was just my cousin." I paused for a
minute, then accused, "You could have asked her to the
dance too, you know."

Farren did not even look up. Wryly I conceded,
"Besides that, we've failed to save her in the past twice
now. And every single interaction we have with anyone,

especially those who know us, compounds the chances that we will be found out eventually."

Farren knew that, but I could see the determination on his face. "Okay. How about this?" he suggested, "We jump back to the day of the wreck … this morning. You call Ellen and tell her you're not feeling well and mention that I don't have a date." In a poor imitation of my voice, he said, " 'Maybe Farren can stand in for me.' If she doesn't want to go with me, I get that. But at least she wouldn't leave the coffee shop mad and drive … you know, dangerous."

I considered his idea and appreciated his selfless expectation of being rebuffed, third-party. It did have merit, but it also had a few giant problems, which I pointed out. "Now I have to completely lie to her, in order to save her from herself. And you may have to take her to the dance, in full knowledge of the future and all of our time jumping. You will have to interact with a roomful of kids from back then. Well, now. 1996. You know what I mean. Anyway, you will have to be the best actor in history to pull off a seamless performance. Otherwise, we can bank on people like Khatri spotting us and hunting us down."

"Maybe, you can jump back and leave me in our natural time zone when you tell her that. Then I would be unaware of what was happening, and I could proceed as normal," Farren offered.

My head was spinning with the potential disaster. "In that scenario, I call her and lie. Then I call you and lie. Then, proceeding as normal, means we're banking on the eighteen-year-old version of the guy, who incidentally doesn't have the confidence to ask her out after twenty more years, to pick up the mantle and run with it."

"Do we have a better plan?" he snapped in challenge.

I shook my head to the negative, and just then the phone rang. We both jumped and a chill of expectation swept over me. My stomach felt suddenly sick, and I held my breath until I heard Mrs. Helton call down the stairs in a concerned voice, "Farren. It's for you."

The hair on the back of my neck stood up as Farren hesitantly reached for the phone. We both knew what the call was about. And we both were stricken by its difference. I had received the call and I had called Farren when it happened the original time. Our tampering had not solved the problem, but had already changed history, and there were undoubtedly results that were yet to be seen. I reached for our cell phones even as Farren answered the landline phone on the end table.

When he answered it, his face went pure white. "He's right here," he muttered thickly, and he handed the phone to me.

I was struck by how heavy the handset was for the old style phone as I brought it to my ear. "This is Chad," I heard myself say.

Plan B

I heard a voice say, "Chad, I've been in a bad car wreck."

My head felt suddenly light and I gasped, "Who is this?"

"Ellen. I've been in a bad car wreck and can't get ahold of Dad or Mom. Our phone must be down," she replied.

"Where are you?" I asked.

"I'm at the hospital," she replied.

"What happened?" I choked out, trying to control my voice.

"It's been the worst night ever. Pouring rain, like, you couldn't see anything. Then some crazy almost hit me at an intersection. Then he almost ran over some homeless guy. Then he hit a cop car and the cop got him off the road.

"Then I got behind a huge old truck that was going way too slow. Then he slams on his brakes at the train crossing! And I crashed into him, and I think I totaled mom's car. She's gonna kill me.

"The crossing bar thing and the lights didn't come down and that train came through there and that old guy in the truck almost got hit by the train. The airbag blew up in my face and I may need surgery on my knee." Ellen's story came out in a torrent of random flurry.

"Chad ... are you crying?" she asked.

"I'm just glad you didn't get killed," was all I could choke out. I looked at Farren and he was a mess too.

Ellen asked, "Can you get your mom or dad to come sign me out of the hospital? I told them I was three days from turning eighteen and they said I still have to have an adult relative check me out."

"I'm an adult. I'll be right over," I said.

"You've got to be over twenty-one," she replied.

"Well, I'm a long way past that ..." The look of alarm on Farren's face alerted me to my gaff. Awkwardly I finished with, "in my mind anyway. I'll get my parents and we'll be there as fast as we can."

I made to hang up the phone, but just before the handset touched the receiver, I pulled it back to my ear and said, "Hey, Ellen. Are you still there?"

I heard a nurse say something, and Ellen came back on the phone, "Are you still here?" she asked.

"Yeah. Is it all right if I bring Farren?" I asked.

"Um, my hair's a mess and they have this brownish yellow stuff on my face where the thingy from the middle of the steering wheel smacked me," she said tentatively.

"Okay. That's no problem, I'll bring him. He's been worried sick," I replied and dropped the phone into the receiver before she could counter.

"She doesn't want me there," he said immediately. The long term hope he had held onto for decades had been shattered in one rejection. He looked forlorn.

I thought, *What would Tanya say here?*

"Nope. You're coming with. She was worried about her appearance. That's a good sign, Farren," I insisted.

It seemed like it took a long time to get to my house, pick up my mom, and make it to the hospital. Farren and I were both nervous about being in close proximity to my mom, but she was so preoccupied with Ellen's situation that she hardly seemed to notice us.

When we got to the emergency room, they amazingly allowed us all into the room with Ellen. My mom, after hugs and tears and hearing the story from Ellen, went to the desk, and began the lengthy sign-out process. I thought, *This is ridiculous! I've broken out of prisons easier than this.*

As soon as mom was gone, I blurted out, "I'm really sorry about the whole dance thing. I was just really humiliated by what they did to us."

Ellen shrugged. "I know. I just wanted to show them we weren't going to be stopped by their cruel jokes."

I shook my head and muttered, "I'm just sorry. Really sorry. And I can't tell you how thankful I am that you're alive."

"Well, I can't dance now anyway. Not with eighteen stitches in my left knee," she said with a dejected shrug.

Farren suggested, "Hey, you could dress as a patient, and ride on one of these stretchers. And Chad and I could dress in hospital scrubs and wheel you around the dance. We'd show those knuckle-dragging buffoons who's not going to be stopped from having fun."

I was aghast at his idea, but Ellen giggled so hard I knew an intervention was necessary. "Yeah. About that. I bet **history** would remember that a lot, Farren. A lot."

He immediately caught my meaning and retracted with, "But, we'd best let you recuperate. Maybe we could come by and play Mancala."

Ellen practically glowed at the suggestion, and I wondered how many clues like that I had missed in my life.

When my mom was finally able to spring Ellen from the hospital, we took her directly home. At the railroad crossing, the cars had been removed. The only remaining vestige of the wreck was a patrol car with its lights flashing and a few flares on the road. I recognized the officer as the one who had pulled me over. He was diligently posted on the tracks with a flashlight waving us across. I wondered how long it would take for the repair crew to come fix the signal. The officer looked weary, and I felt a twinge of guilt. *Odd*, I thought, *this is one of the few things that is entirely not my fault. And I still feel guilty.*

It was late by the time we left Ellen's house. We dropped Farren off at his home, and we made it home sometime after midnight. As soon as I got into my room,

Farren texted, "For the record, I don't think her death was your fault. She wasn't as angry as she should have been. I just think she was messed up by the storm. Anyway, what's our Plan B now?"

I responded, "I don't know. I think I should warn my parents that I may be getting a ticket in the mail. I'm not sure how I will handle that if I don't remember the event. How are we going to remember to bring the Mancala board to Ellen's tomorrow? Are you going to ride this out? Or do we jump back home and see what happened?"

His response was a bit cryptic. "I have a foreshadowing. It's like the memory of a dream. Is that weird or creepy to you?"

I replied, "I have a similar sense that I got a warning ticket in the mail. But that hasn't happened yet. Is it possible that our subconscious is drafting memories from our organic time? Like a download with a really slow connection?"

His reply expressed my sentiments perfectly. "I'm freaked out right now. Let's jump home and, if nothing has changed, we can regroup. Maybe, if everything is all right, we can burn the program for real now."

As much as I had pressed for that exact thing, I was not quite ready to terminate our program. I texted back, "You jump home. I'll meet you there ten minutes after we jumped out. I have one more thing to fix." Then I hit the jump button. I had been contemplating it for some time.

When I landed in my dorm room, everything looked right. That was a relief. I hurriedly changed into my own clothes of that era, and headed for the computer lab. *One more wrong to right,* I mused to myself. *Then we can dispose of time travel forever.* I felt like Frodo climbing up Mount Doom to discard the ring. Only there was no epic music.

I successfully navigated the campus without having any significant contact with students or staff. When I took my place on my lab chair in the empty office, I was once again the teacher's aid ready to pass judgment on the freshmen students.

The professor, Dr. Dahl, had required a vision statement from each freshman student at the beginning of the semester. What he wanted was for the students to think outside the box about how they could use computer technology in their respective fields.

I took the papers from my out-box, and carefully read their vision statements, then read my responses. Some of the students had actually articulated some pretty good vision statements. Others had obviously struggled with anything imaginative. My responses varied appropriately.

When I came to Tanya's, I set it aside and saved it for last. When at last I held it with trembling hands, I read:

I plan to be a relationship counselor and coach. My life goal is to better the world by teaching people to effectively interact to develop a deep level of commitment through open and honest communication. I think using Internet technology for live connections with loved ones who are far away (i.e. deployed military spouses and parents) has potential to counteract much of their loneliness and can become a great tool. I have never had much luck with computers. That's why I signed up for this class.

I had obviously not been impressed with the warm fuzzy tenor of her note. All of the others had been much more technical in nature and I had identified with them easily.

My mind flitted to a brief conversation I had with Tanya, as it was, in the future. Her father was black, and had been raised in a poor neighborhood in Charleston, South Carolina. He had joined the Navy to get an education and make a better life for himself. Her mother was Japanese, and they had met in Okinawa when he was stationed there. Their life had been typical of military families, until one deployment when he had come home under a flag.

I shamefully read the stinging criticism I had penned across the top of that paper. In a technical sense, it had only been minutes before, but from my life perspective, it had taken place about half my lifetime prior. I was embarrassed beyond description.

I looked at my phone, set the time, grabbed all of the papers except Tanya's, and jumped back an hour. Tanya's paper magically appeared in my in-box.

I dropped the rest of the papers into my out-box and felt the tiniest twinge of guilt at not having to redo all of the papers.

When I picked up Tanya's paper, I was relieved to see that my response was not there. "Time's the best eraser," I muttered to myself in amusement. Then I wrote across the top of the paper, *I have no doubt that you will make the world a better place. If you need any help with your computer labs or assignments, feel free to contact me.*

I was just about to put her paper back into the out-box, when I decided to add my phone number.

My palms were sweaty when I jumped back to my organic time. I landed in my recliner like a boss and thought, *Too bad that was the last time jump of history. I've finally mastered the landing.*

I reclined back and, for the first time in decades, I fell asleep easily.

Wake-up Call

I was startled awake by a hand tapping my arm. "Dad, wake up. Mom said you need to hurry and get ready or we'll be late."

As my eyes focused on my ten-year-old son, my mind felt like it was coming out of a bucket of tar. It was the last science fair of Cody's grade school career, and I knew he had all ambitions of going out with a bang. I certainly did not want to miss that.

He asked, "Dad, were you dreaming?"

"Um, I guess so," I muttered. "Why, was I snoring or something?"

"Your feet were twitching like the dog's when he dreams," Cody replied with a snicker.

"Maybe I was dreaming about dog treats," I joked as I headed for the bedroom to get changed.

As I walked into our bedroom, Tanya said, "The babysitter has appendicitis, so I've arranged for Ellen to watch Thaddeus. When we drop him off, Farren will ride over to the science fair with us."

"Okay ...?" Hesitantly I asked, "Isn't Caroline sick?"

Shaking her head, Tanya replied, "Fever has been gone for twenty-four hours, and the doctor says she's not contagious. Ellen says her appetite is back in full swing, so she and Thaddeus should have a blast."

"Humpf. Have a blast, eating them out of house and home," I chuckled.

My mind raced through life, and I realized that I had dreamed the whole time jumping escapade. It had seemed so real, but my entire life story was tangible and standing before my eyes. The conflict left me with a befuddled sense of reality. I had never dreamed in such vivid details. It made me concerned that I might be experiencing symptoms of an early onset of some form of dementia.

Tanya cut into my thoughts with, "Baby, could you zip me?"

I worked the obstinate zipper of her dress up, and my heart skipped a beat. The scar was big, and it was obviously an exit wound scar. I gingerly touched it, and mentally gasped.

"It's still there, Baby. Just like every other time," Tanya said in her matter-of-fact tone.

I finished zipping the dress as I replied, "That moment still haunts my dreams."

She turned and embraced me. "I'm glad I don't remember any of it," she whispered. "And, I'm glad you still don't regret saving me."

As we drove to the science fair, I pondered what Tanya had meant by not remembering. But I did not have a chance to discuss it with her. My own memories seemed to be at such diametric conflict in my mind, I was unsure of what reality actually was. Farren acted strangely, and I wondered if he was dealing with the same kind of PTSD. *Had we actually jumped around in time and, in so doing, changed our lives dramatically? Or was I confused by a graphic dream? Was I mixing reality with a dream to such a level of confusion that my mind was not differentiating between the two? Had I actually lived two unique realities? Should I check in with a psychologist, other than my wife, to determine if I was crazy?*

I did not want to say anything that would alarm Tanya, so I kept my thoughts to myself.

At the science fair, each of the students set up their displays, and I was particularly proud of how Cody had set his up. I knew the teacher had coached him, but he had done a lot of research in the area of how light affects the brain. His postulation was that brain trauma could be more effectively healed with natural light cycle therapy. As I read through his display and pressed the interactive buttons, I wondered if I should spend more hours in natural light.

Tanya squeezed my arm at that moment, and I wondered if she was reading my mind. Ironically I thought, *If she is, that's better than I'm doing.*

"Maybe we should plant a garden," I suggested.

Tanya nodded in agreement, and I again wondered, *Am I crazy and everyone else knows it? Or is she thinking we need to improve our natural light exposure as a preventative measure?*

I concluded that pondering those things assured that I was not suffering from dementia. But, it did not reassure me about my sanity.

After the lunch break, Cody's teacher, Mr. Nichols, asked me into his office. Another one of the judges that I did not recognize was in the office as well. "Dr. Thompson," Nichols greeted as he closed the door. "This is Dr. Clayton, professor of neuroscience at Harvard Medical School. He is profoundly interested in your son's remarkable work."

I nodded, wondering where the conversation was going. *The kid's ten*, I thought, *He's not going to Harvard at this age. I don't care what.*

Mr. Nichols continued, "It's obvious that Cody has taken after his father in his scientific research abilities. But we have a slightly different topic to discuss with you."

He handed me a paper with the date April 28, 1945, and a set of GPS coordinates. I studied the coordinates as my mind raced to figure out the mystery. I slowly said, "This must be somewhere in Europe, maybe Poland. But I don't know about the date." I looked up as I asked, "Are there any other clues or notes ... ?"

I was shocked to be staring down the barrel of a pistol in the hand of Mr. Nichols. "Close. It's Berlin, Dr. Thompson. Two days before the death of the Third Reich. You and I are going to remedy the greatest miscarriage of history. So, you'll very carefully take out your phone and take us there now."

My mind flashed around trying to rearrange my memory. *So, it was all real!* I mentally exclaimed. *How did this guy figure it out?* My face felt numb as I stammered, "Kill me now. I'll never do it."

"You're not the one who is going to die, Dr. Thompson," Nichols replied soothingly. He nodded toward a supply room door. Through a small window in the door, I could see Cody messing with his phone, and Tanya leaning in to see his screen.

Nichols continued, "Your wife and son will be comfortable here with an associate of ours. But in exactly one hour, Dr. Clayton will visit them and ... let's just say, you can only afford to waste fifty-nine minutes stalling." He gave a little smile and tilted his head in what was probably supposed to be a disarming gesture. His smile was anything but genuine. "If you do not cause any trouble, you and your family can live happily ever after." Nichols' face hardened in anticipation and he demanded, "Deal?"

With a sigh, I looked down at my phone. *I hope Farren has his tracker thing turned on*, I thought. Carefully I entered the location and date for the jump, then, taking a final look at my wife and son, I asked Nichols, "You ready?"

He had not let go of my arm, and I could feel the pistol against the back of my head. The instant before I pressed the jump button, I saw Tanya and Cody vanish.

The End